Ghosts of the Grave

Copyright © 2012 Michael Sortino

All rights reserved.

ISBN: 1478222093
ISBN-13: 978-1478222095

Ghosts of the Grave

Teddy Gyros: Kid Vampire Slayer

Book Two

MICHAEL SORTINO

This Book Belongs to:

Veronica Pal

To my son who inspired Teddy,
and my brother who inspires me each day.

CONTENTS

	Acknowledgments	i
1	Before the Fall	1
2	Pride Cometh	5
3	Okay, Here Comes the Fall	10
4	Pain Hurts	16
5	That's Not a Nurse!	20
6	Enemies at Home	24
7	Who's Afraid of the Big, Bad Ghost?	30
8	Back in the Jungle	36
9	Not Him Again!	41
10	Ghosts Scare People. Bottom Line!	49
11	Another Epic Fail, But Who's Counting Anyway?	59
12	Time to Get on Your Horse, Son	66
13	Back in the Battle	74
14	Dangers in the Dark	81
15	Darker Plans Come to Light	87
16	A Triple Threat	91
17	Will the Real Vampire Please Step Forward?	103
18	Things That Make You Go Boom!	112
19	When Spirits Collide – You Better Have Insurance!	119
20	Digging Out and Digging In	120

ACKNOWLEDGMENTS

Special thanks to my wife and children who make each day a joy and adventure, to my family for all their support; and to God who writes the best mysteries . . .

1
BEFORE THE FALL

Yes, I took a frightening fall. But, if you want to know the truth, the scariest part of the night came when I realized the heavy breathing in the darkness wasn't my own. You're just not prepared for that, even if you are sneaking around in places you probably shouldn't be.

Next, came the saliva. I didn't know whose it was, only that I had put my hand right in a chilled, gooey puddle of it. *What in the--?!*

I didn't think Shilah had a drooling problem. Maybe, like the rest of us, this sweet and brilliant-beyond-her-years, sixth grader slobbered a bit in her sleep. But she definitely was not sleeping next to me in the darkness. In fact, a good part of the horror I felt at the moment came from the fact that she was, at the time, missing.

Then, the growl came, low and inhuman. And all the details

came together to form a nightmarish reality. *There's a very big, very angry, drooling dog, and it's very close to me!*

A flash of supernatural light lit the tunnel as my gift kicked in and showed me that things were even worse than that. I call it a gift, that special ability to see lurking evil that others usually can't see, but sometimes I didn't think it was. However, in this case, it helped me to see that the wolf-like dog, nearly one and a half times my size with snarling knife-teeth, was not only ferocious, but evil too, emanating a blood-red glow around it. Hounds of hell anyone?

No thanks!

I took off running, back the way I had come. The beast panted after me. I knew I couldn't scream. I couldn't let anyone know we were there. I also knew that I wouldn't survive. How could I outrun this monstrous mass of menacing muscles and fangs?

Plunging through the dark, I wished I had my flashlight, but it was nestled in my backpack under my bed back home. It was cozied up next to the rest of the items I had assembled but failed to take with me that night: a notepad, pens, digital voice recorder, two high-powered walkie-talkies, first aid supplies and, of course, a newly sharpened wooden stake with a crossbeam at its top. I would've given anything for the water bottle tucked into the front pouch, too. A splash of holy water in this charging canine's eyes certainly couldn't hurt.

Now, the reason I forgot to bring my vampire slaying-mystery-solving kit that night was pretty much the same reason Shilah was missing, too. I hated to admit it, but it came down to my pride, and was basically all my fault.

You see, believe it or not, Teddy Gyros (that's me, in case you haven't realized by now), had gotten proud, arrogant, cocky. Call it what you want, but my head, for some alien reason, had grown at least two sizes too big after the success of my incident with Mrs. Withers.

So, when Shilah appeared in the street below that night to tell me that another librarian was missing from our small town of Witowpitee's only library (and one with an unfortunate history of losing its chief workers), it didn't take me long to solve the mystery.

At least, that's what I had thought.

"Go home, Shilah!" I had told her after we had discussed it for a while. "Let the police do their work tonight, and we'll figure this out tomorrow. No biggee. We work better when rested!"

"But, Teddy—" her voice squeaked.

"Hey! Really, I got this!" I told her from high up in my attic room through my own personal window to the world. If only I knew back then just how much I didn't have this! "There's no point in rushing into things," I told her. "Goodnight, Shilah!"

"Good—night," she sighed, her voice heavy with disappointment.

I closed the window and then, after peeking to make sure that she had fully trudged herself away, I hurried to sneak out the back door of my house—my haste, of course, making me forget my backpack!

So, why on earth would I lie to my newly-found best friend in the world, you ask? I honestly don't know. Do you ever do something and then think, *Wow! Did I really just-- Why did I do that?!*

Looking back, I realize the brutal truth: I was out to prove something. Me, the guy who could see vampires and had turned Mrs. Withers' life around. Yes, I still had something to prove.

I'm embarrassed to admit it, but here it is. I wanted to show everyone, but mostly myself, that I didn't need anyone's help to solve anything. I certainly didn't need a little girl to hold my hand anymore.

So, I had snuck out of the house and pedaled as fast as I could to the library on Main Street, past the statue of the ever-watching and ever-weird Civil War soldier, and made my way to the entrance.

Yellow, police tape stretched across the open library door, and one car was parked up front. It belonged to a detective I was sure, but not worried, because he was fast asleep in the front seat, starting his own drool collection.

Perfect conditions for me to snoop around.

So, with a smug little smile, I had slipped under the caution-crime scene tape and moved to the section I thought for sure would hold my answer. What it held, instead, was a surprise that almost made my heart stop.

2
PRIDE COMETH

You see, when Shilah had told me the news, I instantly remembered the dreamy look on the face of that young librarian we had seen just a couple days before, the one who was following what looked like a book floating in mid-air. Even after we ran into her moments later, she still was smiling and giddy-looking.

It could only mean one thing: she was in love. But not the kind that parents seem to be in, the long-lasting, "Hey I know you'll always leave your dirty socks on the side of the bed no matter how many times I tell you, but I love you anyway"-type love. It was another kind that I had seen far too many times before when my sixteen-year old sister, Alexia, had a new crush at school or had discovered some boy pop star to fall for.

She was always all giggles and gazes, just like Miss Lucy, the newly-missing librarian had been on the day we saw her last.

So, here was my bullet-proof theory, soon to be shot down: The section she had seemingly vanished in during our first encounter was none other than the Romance section. Clearly, she had stumbled upon some enchanted book (you know, the floating one) no doubt inhabited by some legendary vampire who had found a way to suck her into the story with him. Boom. Presto-disappear-o!

All I had to do was use my special powers to find the book and—

"Ahhh!" It was at this point that I ran into the heart-stopping surprise as I rounded the edge of the tall bookshelf to enter the paperback lovey-dovey stacks.

Standing there, arms folded and facing me defiantly—was Shilah. Now, don't get me wrong. The girl is far from freaky or scary-looking. I just didn't expect in my wildest dreams that she would be poised there, waiting for me.

"Quiet, Teddy!" she whispered harshly. "We don't want to wake Detective Philips."

"We—I—You—" I stammered. "What are you doing here? I didn't tell you—and there's no way you could've followed me!"

"I think I know you pretty well by now. You had that gleam in your eye, Theodore, and I didn't think you'd be able to sleep tonight without checking things out first. Of course, what better place to start than the last place we both saw Miss Lucy and her weirdly buoyant book."

"Yes," I said, starting to feel offended by this girl's know-it-all attitude. "I was right about to—"

"Here it is," she said, holding forth the very same hard-bound book we'd seen the other day. There was no doubt about it. It had the deep, cherry-wood-like cover with intricate swirls and carvings etched into the edges and binding. I wouldn't have missed it anywhere.

Of course, Shilah didn't miss it either, and this was the

topper for me. I was really angry now. "You know, Shilah," I said, nodding superiorly. "I appreciate you doing the legwork here, but I think I can handle this now. You've done well." I reached authoritatively for the volume.

She pulled it back and clung to it protectively. "Excuse me?"

"I need to see that."

"Yes?"

"Now. Without you."

"No way."

"Just hand it over, like a good assistant," I said, with a beckoning gesture. I knew, deep down, that this last comment would be the doozy for her.

"Assistant!?"

"Shilah, keep your voice down—very unprofessional of you—you'll wake the detective!"

Things got a little fuzzy after this. Mainly because she held up the book and said, "Here!" and, when I stepped forward to grab it, she hit me over the head with it. Thud!

I decided to sit down after this. Well, it was more like my body decided for me. And, any place would do, even the spot I was standing at. Who needs a chair, anyway? They're so old-fashioned!

Okay, yes, my legs buckled out from under me as everything went cloudy, and the next thing I knew I was sitting on the floor with a huge book being dumped into my lap. "Oomf!"

"There you go, sir! Anything else you need, sir, just let me know!" she fumed, her gold-green eyes nearly aflame. I'd never seen Shilah so angry. "I'll be out back following up on one of my terribly inferior hunches, sir. Don't let me get in your way!"

With that, she stormed off.

Well, that was easy. I waited until I thought she was gone for the second time that night, and then cracked open the book. "Here we go," I whispered to myself, feeling the drum roll rumbling through every cell of my body with mounting anticipation. I looked at the title page.

Minnesota Mining – A Non-Illustrated Yet Highly Factual History.

Okay. As it turned out, there wasn't anything special about the book. In fact, it was just a book about the history of mining in our state. And, as the title made a point to point out, it was a very drab and boring one at that.

"Hmm," I said to myself. "Not even romance, and I don't think I'll find a vampire fishing for gold flecks in here." I closed the big book.

Then, a new thought hit me and I decided to check the bookshelf. Maybe there was a hidden lever, like in all the good mysteries, that would make the bookshelf unlatch and reveal a hidden passageway behind it. Of course, it would be triggered by one of the books. One like – "This!" I pulled a book out dramatically. Nothing happened.

Nothing, except for the fact that Teddy Gyros, the great vampire slayer, was standing in an empty library holding a fresh copy of "Puppy Love in Princess Land." I quickly replaced it before Shilah or anyone else saw me.

Twenty minutes, no secret passage discovery and over two-hundred books later, I leaned exhausted against the shelf, marveling at how many guys on the covers of these stories seemed to either have shirts with faulty buttons or a strong enough composition to not need a shirt at all.

This was more challenging than I thought it would be. *And, where is "that girl" anyway? She could've been helping me!* I decided to go out back and give her a piece of my mind.

It was a big piece of my nightmare that I would walk right into, instead. Remember, the evil dog?

Yep, that's coming right up.

3
OKAY, HERE'S THE FALL
(THANKS FOR WAITING)

Hurrying through the forested area behind the library, my black, sweat-jacket got caught on some thorny vines around the base of a pine tree. I pulled it free, hearing a slight tear and grumbling to myself. *Mom's not gonna be happy about that.* And, naturally, it was all Shilah's fault.

Where is she? Doesn't she know about the "buddy system?" Wow. So naïve, so young, assistants these days! Can you believe my attitude? Looking back, I hardly can. Of course, when you set yourself up so high, you're bound to take a big fall, right? I wish someone had warned me of that fact sooner.

"Shilah!" I called out, but not too loudly.

There was a full-faced moon scowling down at me that night, but you would hardly have known it in the shadow-filled patch of trees that I crossed. I knew, from memory, that there was a supply shed on the other side of these trees at the top of the hill. Maybe she had gone there to look for signs of the missing librarians.

Or, maybe she'd just gone home without telling me, to spite me. *I wouldn't put it past her. Girls can be so emotional.*

"Eee!" I screamed, just like a girl, much to my self-horror. I had stepped on something squishy and realized it was a cat, a dead one. Even in the dark I could tell, and I certainly didn't want to hang around and figure out how it had died.

So, I hurried on and came to the shed. It was half-lit by the horizon-pinned moon. In front, like giant teeth, were double doors wide enough for riding mowers or equipment carts to drive through. One of those doors was open.

"Pssst," I said, hanging back in the cover of the last few trees, not wanting to expose myself to whomever or whatever might be hovering around the tin-roofed shack.

There wasn't a trace of the girl. *Couldn't she have left a trail? Even Gretel was smart enough to do that! Yeah, it must've been Hansel's idea!*

"Shi—" I started to call again, when something caught my eye, though I wished it would've missed it completely, such was the fright it sent shrieking down my spine.

A reddish glow appeared in the dirt-clouded, slightly cracked window of the shed, and then vanished. I tried to convince myself that I had imagined it. Then I tried to explain it away. A falling star, reflected in the highly unreflective glass. And a red one, at that. *Hey, maybe the planet Mars was falling!* No, that wouldn't be good.

I made an all-out dash for the edge of the shack to the right of the doors, right around the corner from the window. Panting like a dog in the dark, I made my plan: Get in, make sure Shilah wasn't in there, and get the heck out as fast as humanly possible. Or, if she was in there, grab her and go.

But first, a peek through the dust-distorted glass. Too dark inside, nothing to see. I would have to let the light in from the door, enough to check out the shed.

I ducked under the window and skimmed the wall to the doors. I came to the one that was already opened a foot or so. I pushed it in, gritting my teeth at the groaning sound it made.

I waited. But there was no following sound. No reaction from Shilah or anyone else inside.

Was I feeling an evil presence there? It was hard to tell. There was a great deal of fear surrounding me, not to mention pride inside of me, and these may have been blocking my ability to see things clearly. Maybe it was just a homeless person inside the shack lighting a small fire in the mid-Autumn cold, I told myself. Or, maybe not.

I looked inside. Shapes in the shadows were either monsters or machines, tool-benches and toolboxes or terrifying beasts. No fire, no sign of life. I walked in further, and then the ground disappeared beneath me and I fell—about five feet into musty, dirty darkness.

"Ah!"

I hit the hard ground beneath me and rolled a little into a passage connected to this pit that I had plunged into. (Don't worry. This isn't the incredible fall I've been referring to. The big one is coming. Hang in there!)

Of course, I didn't even have a chance to hang onto anything at the time. I had felt the scrape of dangly, groping tree roots across my back just before I slammed into the floor of the secret passage, but there wasn't a chance of using these to stop the fall.

Thankfully, I wasn't too hurt. Just a bit bruised, physically and ego-wise, too. How could I not have seen the hole in the ground? Was it always there? That's gotta be inconvenient. "Bob, hand me that wrench, will ya? Oh and watch out for that--! Oops."

No, the only answer was that this pit had been secret, it had been covered, but then someone left it uncovered either on purpose or accidentally, and that's how I had found it.

At this point, I tried to funnel the flood of questions in my mind down to two main streams of thought: Where did the passage lead to and, am I going to die? Yes, I admit, I was afraid. Excited, too. Don't get me wrong.

It's not every day that you fall into a secret tunnel. Sometimes you step off a curb without noticing it, and you look ridiculous, like you're doing a weird dance to a song no one else can hear. Or, you're playing a sport on the field and you step into a dip in the grass and tumble like a human soccer ball; but secret tunnels—these are a rare fall-causing find.

So, I had a decision to make. Face my fear of the unknown, of the uncertainty of safety, of being on my own (truth be told, I wished Shilah was there with me) and explore the tunnel, or turn around and climb back up the way I had swiftly and ungracefully come.

Then, another thought hit me. What if my friend, in her anger over how I was treating her, had decided to explore this tunnel on her own? What if she had gotten trapped down here herself and was desperately hoping that I would find her?

That settled it. I needed to explore the tunnel, come what may. It was a suffocating darkness that I started to crawl through, the hard-packed earth moist on my palms and fingers, knees dampening deeper as I moved forward. I could've stood and walked, but, for some reason, crawling just felt safer in the dark.

I went for a few minutes at least, but there was nothing, no light, no sign of Shilah or anyone else; just increasing wetness.

That was why I didn't notice the puddle of saliva at first.

But the heavy breathing, as you remember, was what struck me, there in the void, as utterly terrifying. Add in a healthy helping of evil dog drool, the flash of red-tinted vision and you're back to the beginning of my tale watching the great kid vampire slayer, Teddy Gyros, running like his pants were on fire.

*   *   *

I waved my arms in the dark almost like I was doing the breast stroke through the tunnel, but mostly because I didn't want to run right into the wall and bounce back into the jaws of the pursuing paranormal predator.

I hit it hard anyway. And then, I don't know quite how, but I found myself scrambling up the vertical shaft. At first it was clumps of mud and protruding stones and rock that helped me climb. Then, it was the slippery vines I clutched onto and pulled myself up with their capillary claws splintered and spidery enough for me to grasp by the handfuls.

I was out of the hole before I knew it. Up on my feet, I dug my heels for the doorway, buzzing with adrenaline and almost floating on a cloud of elation. I had made it out and hadn't been eaten by the monster behind me!

That's when lightning struck. I paused to look back, entertaining a delirious hope that the wolf-like dog couldn't climb up the same way I had. I was terribly wrong, and I really hated when that happened. It soared up into view, clutching the edge and springing after me.

Panic didn't bother knocking on the door of my brain. It just barged right back in as I slammed through the shed doors and out into the clearing. The beast pounced after me, jagged jowls gleaming in the moonlight.

"Shilah! Shilah!" I screamed, as I took off running down a

slope, away from the town center buildings.

I had no clue where I was going. Just away. Away! And fast, downhill! *Great, great! Speed, boy—don't look back!*

And, I couldn't look back, the slope was getting so steep, I was barreling through the tall grass so rapidly. But, I didn't have to look to know it was on my heels. I knew I was about to feel at any moment that hot, tearing sensation of razor sharp claws digging into my shoulders and scraping down my back as fiery, savage jaws wrapped around my neck from behind to slam me to the ground.

So, it was almost an immediate rush of relief that hit me when I found myself falling for the second time that night. At least the hell-hound hadn't caught me.

But, the ground below wasn't catching me either. *Oh no.* I flailed in the air.

"Noooo!"

I had read about the mining that kept a good deal of the population of Witowpitee employed, seen the soot-covered men and women returning home from work.

Never did I dream, though, that I would stumble through a section of fallen perimeter fencing and find myself falling into the region's largest and deepest open pit mine below.

How's that for a big fall?

4
PAIN HURTS

Why does pain have to be so painful? I'd like to say that I took the agony like a man, but here's the hard truth: I was still just a boy.

And so, after waking up in a hospital bed three days later, finding out that I had received among the list of Latin words for serious ouches and boo-boos, not just a concussion that had kept me unconscious for nearly five hours, but also a shattered leg, I wept like a child.

I cried too, because the pain medication had worn off and I thought that someone was either jabbing my right leg with a jack hammer or running over it continuously with a monster truck.

It was like I was in a tornado of hurt, faces swirling around me, creased with concern, coming in and out of focus: my mother and father, doctors and nurses, even Shilah—thankfully, although I didn't feel much gratitude at the time over her safety.

I found out later, that a bunch of people had already come by to see me, including Old Mrs. Withers and her daughter, my teacher, Mrs. Thorntrop, and even Father McReedy, the grumpy old priest from the church Shilah and I had sought shelter in over a week ago.

But, right now, all I could think about was nothing but "Aaaaah!"

The voice of my mother seemed distant, light years away. "Nurse! Nurse! He needs more medication!"

The steady gaze of my father, with his, "Hang in there, buddy," was like a tree I tried to hold onto before being pulled back into the tempest of torment.

"Ughhh! Ahhhh. It hurts so bad!" was all I could squeeze out, the tears streaming down my face as I tried to writhe and turn, but strong hands pinned me down.

"Hang in there, Teddy. Hang in there."

Then, a sudden rush of calm and everything went black.

*   *   *

Window to the world,
Why was it me?
It could have been anyone.
But you chose me
To see...

"Why?" This was the big question that I wrestled with for the next few days of recovery. Then, I switched to hand-to-hand combat with it for the next day or so. Why!? I would strike out at it, but it would always slap me back, toying with me, as if I had no chance of beating it. It was only after a full ten days in the hospital and when I was about to open an arsenal of explosives against this pestering opponent, that I got an answer.

And, it wasn't the answer I wanted at all.

Although those days in the hospital were foggy to my memory, I did recall people saying things like, "You're lucky to be alive," and "If that mountain of sand hadn't broken your fall—" along with things like, "These things just happen," and "It was just a terrible accident."

But, while somewhat helpful, these words were ultimately flat to me-- especially when the stabbing agony hit, and especially when it was too soon for my next dose of pain medication. I had already undergone four reconstructive surgeries and, while I was on my way to using my leg again, it was going to be a long road back.

During one of these particularly tough times, my dad lowered the boom.

"It's your own fault, Teddy. You know that, don't you?" He said this with a firmness that was stronger than usual. I could almost tell that he was working very hard not to be compassionate. "If you hadn't been out there, doing God-knows-what, all alone in the middle of the night, you wouldn't be in this mess—your mother—all of us, wouldn't have had this nightmare to go through—almost losing you. Do you know how difficult--? Do you realize what you've done?"

I couldn't answer. Pure sadness gripped my throat, drowned my vocal cords. I looked away from his golden brown eyes, his face that seemed older, hair greyer than I last remembered. I willed with every ounce of strength left inside of me, to keep the tears at bay.

"You're asking why. 'Why did this have to happen to me?'" he went on. "But I think you already know the answer, don't you, Ted? You play with fire, you—you dance on the edge of a mountain—" he shook his head, as if not satisfied with what was coming out of his mouth. "You know what I'm saying, right? You brought this on yourself."

And this, maybe, was the greatest pain of all.

That night, even though it was his turn to stay with me at the hospital while my mom was with the rest of the kids at home, I asked that Mom stay instead. Was it because I was mad at him for what he said? No. I was mad at myself. But the disappointment that I knew was lurking behind his looks at me made that feeling a hundred times worse.

Something else came lurking that night too, and unfortunately it wasn't an emotion.

5
THAT'S NOT A NURSE!

He clung to the doorframe of my hospital room like a poisonous vine, Finnius Ardmyre, long before I even knew he was there. He was so tall that he had to hunch over, his nose pointed down like a long thorn, his groping fingers like clutching claws of sickly vegetation.

But, why was he here, the second and least popular of our two town morticians? He prepared the dead for burial. He dealt in death.

Was this why children scattered like bugs when he strode down the sidewalk? Or was it because they sensed something more in his smug, pasty-lipped smile, something else behind his narrow, dark eyes, something calculating, like he was always measuring you up, determining just the right coffin size?

While most people hesitated and dodged a little if they could, he went out of his way, all the kids knew, to step on insects as he took his long strolls through town. He seemed to especially enjoy his early morning walks in front of the elementary school, all shrouded and ominous-looking in his heavy black overcoat. And, in the Spring, when the snails were crawling about, he seemed to take particular pleasure in crushing these helpless slime-merchants beneath his blood-resistant boots.

Crack! Crack! Crunch! That was a big one!

Maybe he enjoyed the way they sounded, the poor things who couldn't flee fast enough, as he mushed them into goo and shell fragments. Or was it the power to put down his second fiddle and play Death itself, even in this small way that thrilled him?

That's what I thought. He liked his job way too much.

You can understand then, the horror that I felt when I awoke in the middle of the night to see him there. Why was he at my door?

My mother was asleep in the chair next to me. It was three thirteen. She had every right to be asleep. Normal people sleep at these times. Freaky, evil people stand in sick kids' doorways at a time like this.

Where was the remote control with the nurse button on it? I groped among the bed sheets ever-so-slowly and minimally, not wanting him to know that I was awake. My eyes squinting, I couldn't tell if he was coming closer or just standing there, watching me with a sidelong glance.

This, of course, was the same man that appeared to be working with the driver of that mysterious van which had followed Shilah and I on the day we made our mad dash to the church called St. Elizabeth Ann Seton—the one with grumpy, old Father McReedy.

I remembered the feeling that I felt at Betty's Burgers when I saw this undertaker talking to the driver and glancing through the front window at me and my family.

There was no doubt in my mind at the time and especially at this moment, that Finnius Ardmyre was bad news; that, if there was really a battle going on with two sides opposing each other, then he was definitely on one and I was on the other.

Maybe that's why he was there, lit by the pale hallway light behind him, shadowy and sinister-like. He might have a drug or potion which he wanted to put just a drop of in my water or drip with a skinny, long tube into my ear as I slept. And just like that, I would be out of the picture, one less opponent that he had to deal with.

I wanted to scream. I couldn't find the nurse's button. I couldn't even find my voice to squeak out a cry to my mother.

It would only take one stride of his long, tent-pole legs for him to be at my side and over and done with his dastardly deed before anyone could stop him.

He turned now, as if sensing my agitation, even though I was mostly in darkness and he had the light on him. He looked like he was about to enter the room when, quite swiftly, like an angel in white, one of my nurses was there, Gale Summers, and she had him by the arm.

There were low whispers between them, and she was scolding him, like he was a schoolboy, her radiant face flush with righteous anger. Though I could barely hear them, I could pick out her statements, like, "What do you think you are doing?!" and something about visiting hours being long over.

His voice was so low I could scarcely make out his mumbling something about "Making my rounds," and "offering my services."

This seemed to enrage the young woman even more and my heart leapt with both relief and pride as I saw her dispel the phantom-like man with a "You get out of here, Mr. Ardmyre—you know you've been told before! This is the last place you should be, and this is your last warning! If I catch you in the children's ward again, I'll call the police, don't think I won't!"

My mom stirred at these last words.

Ardmyre's eyes caught the light, revealing an indignant flash of anger as he glanced my way, and then, like a storm cloud sucked away by a sudden change in atmosphere, he was gone.

Gale came in with a sigh and moved to my side, adjusting my covers. I closed my eyes completely, wondering if she would notice how fast my heart was still beating. She did seem to notice my sweat-soaked hair on my forehead, and like an Old West gunslinger, she whipped her temperature monitor from its holster on her belt and ran the cold, plastic bulb across my brow before I knew it.

"Is his fever back?" I heard my mother's tender but tired voice ask.

"No, he's fine. He should be able to go home tomorrow, on schedule. Yeah, I knew that was your next question."

"Thank you, Gale."

Yes, thank you, Gale. And, closing my eyes wearily, I thanked God that I was finally going home. What I didn't know at the time was that worse things than Finnius Ardmyre would find me there.

6
ENEMIES AT HOME

They were far less obvious these new enemies that attacked me on my return home. Yes, it was a huge gift to be able to get out of the zoo exhibit, as I liked to call my hospital room. People coming to stop and stare at me, the weird, frozen sense that you're still in the world, that this is life, but in a suspended, different way—how could I not begin to feel like a trapped zebra or lion?

Of course, deep inside I felt more like a dog with his tail tucked between his legs. I had made a mistake, a big one, and, returning home, this reality hit me even harder.

My siblings were caring enough. Doug actually carried me up to my room. And, although I felt very foolish, and two-year old Bobby thought it was fun to try and hang on my one good leg halfway up, causing a near catastrophe, it was a nice gesture. Leah, our six-year old informer, hit me with a status report as Mom got me settled in bed and Dad opened my window to air out the attic room.

"Bobby took your baseball card collection and chewed on each card," she told me with utter seriousness, followed by, "Alexia used your room three nights in a row to talk on the phone—and I think she cried all over your pillow." Then she grinned and pulled out her marker set to start drawing all over the cast which covered my entire right leg.

"What? I-- she--?" I looked in horror to my mother.

She gave a knowing look as she arranged some art supplies from my closet on a new folding table by my bed. "She broke up with Brad—sorry, honey. She needed some space."

"She couldn't go outside? She had to use my room?" I was feeling agitated for a lot of reasons, but this seemed like a good one as any to let people know about it. "She wouldn't let me in her room if my life depended on it. But, when I'm almost dead in the hospital, she just moves in here! I can still smell her. Didn't you wash the sheets?"

"Yes, I did. You're imagining things, Teddy. And, you're not being fair."

Alexia appeared in my doorway at this point, and I could tell that her eyes were red, that she had been crying again. Part of me was sure she had found my favorite Saturday shirt-- the tattered one with the emblem of a knight on the front that I liked to wear on days planned for high adventure—and just wept all over it, maybe even finished with blowing her nose in it. Why wouldn't she?

"Hi, Teddy—sorry," she said. "You doin' okay?"

This was when the other part of me kicked in. She was my sister, after all. Bigger, meaner at times (especially when she was in charge of the house, babysitting, and I apparently drove her crazy); she was utterly and confusingly emotional, yes, but still my sister. "Sorry about Brad," I found myself saying as the protective, caring side won over the injured one. "He smelled like liver sandwiches anyway." It was the best I could do.

She laughed a little as she came to the end of my bed to rest a hand on my good leg. "You're right." She took a red marker from Leah's set and drew a heart on my cast and then signed her name beneath it, "Alexia," in fancy script.

Looking at my parents who watched with cautious, trying-to-be-positive eyes, holding hands in the doorway, I had the sudden, sinking feeling that the zoo exhibit was still in force. It had just been moved to a new location.

The cast, it turned out, needed to be on for six weeks—six more weeks of itchy, immobilized torture! "With any luck," the doctors said, like they were just reading off the weather forecast, "he'll be back to school by Halloween, off crutches by Thanksgiving . . . if this high pressure system holds up."

There was a great deal of pressure, all right, and it wasn't just in my cast. The tough, cruel reality of my limited life settled in quickly and it wasn't long before the first big opponent came knocking on my door—despair.

It was a sneaky one, too. I didn't know I was terribly depressed until much later. At the time I just felt majorly bummed.

I didn't want to draw, didn't want to read, let alone tackle the mounds of missed schoolwork that was steadily piling up. Even the video games and TV shows that were temporarily allowed in my room didn't seem to interest me much.

I couldn't shake this heavy sadness on my heart, for some reason. It was hard to put into words, and I didn't have the energy to even try.

On one afternoon, after Shilah had finished filling me in on the events of another school day I had missed, she tried to get me to fess up.

"What's wrong with you, Teddy?" she asked, perched with

her legs up in a sofa-chair that my Dad had brought in for visitors. She had her school agenda in her lap, having just double-checked that all her homework and studying was finished for the day. She fidgeted with the wire binding, trying to twist the renegade top part back into line with the rest. "You don't care about anything I'm saying, do you?"

I sighed. She was right. But, what could I say? The fact that Chuck had been caught cheating on a math test again and that Cynthia had given a demonstration of her new cell phone for everyone on the playground like a princess displaying a new addition to the crown jewels, just didn't seem to interest me.

It was the same thing, day after day, for nearly four weeks. And the feelings only grew worse.

Even the news reports didn't mean much to me. Mrs. Thorntrop had reported how Mr. Brady Walters put a stop to the excavation that he had begrudgingly allowed at his ranch, and this was causing a bit of an uproar. Apparently, he had given in to the pressure of the more-cultured in Witowpitee, and had agreed to let a team of archeologists start to scope out the area. But now he had changed his mind, having grown angry at how the influx of workers was negatively affecting his cattle and his business. So, for now, the digging in the Indian burial ground was brought to an abrupt stop.

Even a discussion about the missing librarians held little interest for me. We had already talked about all we could, and now we were just stuck, waiting for me to get better, so we could continue investigating.

Early on, like day four of my hospital visit, Shilah and I had decided to tell the police about the mine shaft hidden in the shed on the library grounds. This wasn't something my friend could let me keep secret. People's lives depended on it.

And it wasn't that I didn't care about those lives, I just

didn't want the extra humiliation that would come along with the revelation. Soon everyone would know that Teddy Gyros was out looking for the missing ladies and had failed miserably.

I thought, well, maybe an anonymous note would be better, but Shilah had convinced me that it would at least give my parents and the authorities a reason as to why I was running around the area that night.

Did we think I should tell them about the evil, drool-demon that chased me to my near-death? No, not quite yet.

This was the frustrating part. I knew evil was out there, at play, and there was nothing I could do about it, stuck home, stuck in a plaster prison from hip to toe. "Have the police said anything about the mine tunnel?" I asked Shilah one evening towards the end of the four weeks, as I toyed with a half-eaten plate of macaroni and cheese. The shape of the hardening elbow noodles seemed to form an odd picture to me, like an arrowhead, but I didn't give it much attention.

"No, it didn't pan out. It's blocked off after thirty feet, and some old groundskeeper said that it had been used in the old days for extra storage. Hey, Gary Greystone was on the news again last night," she said with a little roll of her eyes. "You should have seen him."

"All smiles, still?"

"Yeah, with two people missing for over a month, and he just seems to love sitting in the lights and showing his pearly white teeth for the national news stations. Makes me sick."

I could just see it. Mr. Greyson was the library manager who acted more like a movie star promoting his next film than a public service worker. Slicked, black hair, a handsome face that some said rivaled a young Tom Cruise or Mel Gibson, he didn't seem nervous at all when the microphone was pointed his way, and his comments like, "These brave, sweet ladies are in our thoughts and prayers, daily," and "Why did such a tragedy have to strike our little, humble and innocent town, I'll never know, but I won't sleep until it has been made right," turned my stomach when I heard them, they felt so shallow and insincere to me.

"He's such a poser," Shilah declared, sharing my thoughts as she clicked off the TV in my mind. "Cares more about his hairdo than those women, I bet." She clutched her bookbag. "Well, gotta run."

My best friend stood to leave and I felt my heart jump a little. "Don't go!" I wanted to say, but I didn't, couldn't. It was getting late, and it would soon be lights-out time, the worst part of my dismal days stuck at home.

Her parting comment didn't make it any easier. "I gotta go home and call Officer Peters. Detective Phillips said he's going to be ordered to look into the real reason Walters put a stop to the digging at the Indian burial ground, the ghost sightings there—and I wanted to share with him some thoughts I had."

"What—ghosts?!" I exclaimed.

But, like a spirit passing through the door, she was gone.

7
WHO'S AFRAID OF THE BIG, BAD GHOST?

The next morning, I went berserk. You know how you see people just flip out sometimes? Well, maybe not in real life, but in the movies or on TV—they just start throwing things, tip over a table, stuff like that?

Here's what happened. Follow me and you'll understand why I did it.

My mom came in after dropping little Leah off at school. The woman had soft capri pants and a cozy, grey sweater that I used to love snuggling up to her when she wore it, just a year or two ago (okay, even recently—she's my mom!). She smelled like April rain, as always, just glowing with love and total concern for me as she straightened up my mess-heap of a room. She picked up a plate with a half-eaten piece of pie from last night that could better be used as a doorstop today. Then, she freed the personal pizza box that currently held that position and turned to look at me. "So, kiddo, you want some chocolate chip pancakes this morning?" she asked, cheerily.

"That's it!" I shouted, and I just ran my forearm across my nightstand, knocking everything off, water cup, school papers, pirate lamp and all. It all just crashed and spilled and tumbled to the floor as I exclaimed, "How can you say such a thing!?" And I bounced up and down on my bed, furiously trying to work myself to the edge to stand on my good leg. "How!" Bounce! "Can!" Bounce. "You!?" Thump!

I had bounced off all right, landed on the good foot of my good leg and instantly slipped on the water I had just spilled there, causing a rear-end collision with the floor of my room. "Oh! That hurts."

My mom just looked at me with a curious expression on her face and a load of dirty clothes in her arms. "Hmm. Looks like someone could use some fresh air today," was all she said as she backed out of the room and left me there, wallowing in my fury.

Twenty minutes later, I sat in the car parked outside of Dr. Phillips' office. He was the torture specialist who had inflicted this infernal punishment on me, without even one of my loved ones raising a peep to defend me. They just let him put me in this plaster leg-prison for half my life! Now, my mom was inside, picking up my crutches.

I watched the busy people of Witowpitee go by me. We were right in the middle of Main Street and I could see them all: Ladies buzzing in and out of the beauty parlor, hair flat on entry, billowing and pluming on exit; men in overalls spitting tobacco while loading beams from the lumber supply; businesspeople in suits making their ever-important trek from the coffee shop to the court house, none of them pausing to even acknowledge the statue of the Civil War soldier that watched them all go by.

I commiserated with that statue now. I stared at it, feeling almost one with it. Because, that's just how I felt. No one cared a hoot about me, it seemed. They all just went on with their lives as normal, while mine was on hold and I was frozen in time, just like that soldier guy. Of course, I wasn't made of bronze, and I didn't have some strange legend attached to me, whatever it was.

I did get the feeling, however, over the last few weeks, that people were labeling me as "strange" and probably "best to be avoided."

My mom came out, carrying my wooden get-me-arounds, and she opened the sliding mini-van door to put them in. I felt sorry for her as I watched her. My outburst in my room was totally uncalled for, I knew it, and I was about to apologize when she said, "There! Now we can get you around more, and you won't feel so cooped up in that attic!"

A passing elderly woman gave her a look of surprise at this.

"It's a big, attic room," my mom explained. "It's his bedroom, really quite nice."

The greying woman just grinned cautiously and hurried on.

"Hey, you know what, Mom?" I said, as she got into the driver's seat.

"What, Teddy?"

"You're the best."

The next stop was the market, the Park Street Grocery, and I opted to wait in the car again. It wasn't that I was still upset. The fresh air and the change of scenery, not to mention the time with Mom, were actually making me feel a bit better. No, it was just that I was afraid to try my new crutches out in public. I wanted to get some test runs in first, before I made that bold move.

Turns out, I wasn't the only one dealing with fear issues at that moment. The van door opened and I thought it was my mom loading bags from her side, but it closed right away with a clang and I saw, with some surprise, Office Peters sitting on Leah's car seat, in uniform and out of breath.

"Teddy!" he said, winded.

"Officer--!?"

"Peters. Remember, me? Of course you do. How could you forget!?" He grabbed a half-empty apple juice box from the seat pouch in front of him (probably weeks old) and squirted the remaining drink in his mouth. He sighed. "Disgusting, but needed. Whew!"

"What's wrong?" I asked him. "What's going on?"

He looked around the area, eyes wide and alert. "Oh, you might say I'm hiding from some—one."

"Your shadow again?" I hated to bring such a sensitive subject up.

"Oh, no! Not that! I'm fine with my shadow. During the day. Night's another story, but right now I'm hiding from my Captain—whoah, there he is! Duck! No, don't duck! I will!" And he face-planted himself into the narrow gap between the middle seats.

I looked to see a man that I recognized from the papers and the large shiny badge on his chest as Captain Rogers. He stood in a pleated suit in front of the police building in the square opposite the courthouse and adjacent to the library. Scanning. He was definitely scanning with those big, overgrown eyebrows furrowed; but we were at least a hundred yards from him, and he wasn't on the move.

"Don't worry, he's not coming this way," I told Officer Peters, relieved to have at least a little excitement back in my life. "Why are you hiding from him?"

"Well," the early twenties rookie officer looked back at me, unaware that he had two stale gummy bears stuck to his forehead. He was lucky. It could've been a lot worse, going back there head-first. "I just got my assignment in the briefing this morning and I don't want to talk to him about it, that's why."

"What's your assignment?"

"Oh, it's nothing," he laughed, trying to sound dismissive. "Just need to investigate the ghost sightings at the Walter's Ranch, that's all."

At this moment, there was a loud bang on the hood of the van.

"Ahh!" the young man screamed, high-pitched, burying his face again.

I spun to see nothing. Then, a husky, huge man with a bushy beard straightened up in front of the van, picking up a large volume, the one he had apparently dropped onto the hood. The book was very thick and looked heavy. It was a wonder there was no dent left behind.

But the man had a nervous look in his wide, grey eyes when they caught mine. Maybe it was because he thought I was going to tell my mother on him. But there seemed to be something more, something unusual, like he recognized me or something.

Then, from Dusty Pages, the antique book shop two stores down, a clerk came running. "Mr. Gorgenstein, you forgot your cookbook!"

Looking even more alarmed now, and hoisting the massive hardback under one arm, he quickly stormed over to nearly barrel into the clerk and snatch the thin, dusty-looking book from his hands with a German-heavy bark, "It's no cookbook, fool!" And, then he hurried to pass my van again, staring at me once more before jumping into a mud-covered jeep and peeling out of his parking spot and down Main Street.

Officer Peters peeked his head back up now with an additional gummy bear over each eye. "What was that about?"

"I don't know," I said, wanting to tell him that the second book, the thin one, had sent off some interior alarms inside of me, and I was just registering an eeriness about it as the burly Gorgenstein slipped it into his overcoat and charged away. "Probably nothing," I assured him, clearing my throat. "Hey, you don't really believe that there are such things as ghosts," I told him, trying to bring the conversation back around to where we'd left it.

Peters began picking the gummy bears off his face, one by one, nervously eating them as he answered. "Teddy, Teddy. You're the new guy here, I know, but that don't mean you're dumb, I can tell. You're a sharp one. You, uh, ran into me that night a little while back, and I know, from what I hear, you've seen stranger things around here. But, if you've seen what I've seen in my day, you'd step right up and gladly take that ticket for the believing-in-ghosts train. Believe me."

"What have you seen, Officer Peters?" was all I could ask, hoping we wouldn't be interrupted again. I was dying to know his story, but, as it turned out, "dying" was a very poor choice of words.

8
BACK IN THE JUNGLE

"Did you ever read the Peter Pan story?" Officer Peters started, carefully, and I nodded as he went on. "I loved that story when I was a kid. Well, my name, you know-- but I really thought I was Peter Pan for years. Just flyin' everywhere. Adventures, sword fighting and fun with my sister and our friends. But then," he hesitated, and I knew the bad part was coming.

I glanced inside the grocery store and noticed that my mom was at the check-out counter. We only had a few minutes. "Go on," I told the young officer who fidgeted with a stale gummy bear.

"My sister got sick," he said. "She didn't have long to live— cancer. And then, that summer, when the fair was in town, I decided, even though my parents always said not to, that I was gonna visit the fortune teller booth. I told the lady behind the curtain what was happening, and she noticed I was dressed like Peter Pan. I was still little-- 8 years old, I think.

"'You really want your sister to live?' she asked me. I said yes, that I'd give anything. And then, she looked at me with this strange little gleam in her eye, almost like she was happy, and she asked, 'Even your shadow?'" Officer Peters stared off now, lost in the memory. "'My shadow?' I asked. 'What do you mean?'

"'Your sister will live,' she told me, 'If you promise to give up your shadow in return, and live in the shadow of death the rest of your life.'

'Yes, yes, anything!' I said, not even realizing what she meant. My dad was looking for me, calling for me, and I didn't have time to think. The old woman reached her hand out, and I took it, thinking she wanted to shake on the deal, you know, but she dug her long fingernail into my palm and quickly took a drop of blood away on the tip of her forefinger, disappearing back behind her curtain, whispering, 'The deal is done!'"

A woman appeared at the van window opposite me at that moment and I nearly jumped out of my skin. "Whoah!" Thankfully, it was my mother. She knocked. The keys were in the ignition, doors locked. I acted like I didn't know what she wanted, needed to buy more time. "What happened?" I asked, turning to Officer Peters.

"My sister," Officer Peters said, still looking off. "She got—she got better. And—"

Knock! Knock! Knock! My mom was a little peeved now.

"And--!?"

"And," he said, blinking now, looking like he saw me again and my mother for the first time. "And, you better let her in," he sighed.

I groaned, pressing the door lock button.

"Sorry, Mrs. Gyros!" Officer Peters jumped out of the van to help her with the bags in her hands. "Did I pronounce that right? I was just telling Teddy a story, that's all. I'm Officer Peters. Just keeping the kiddo company while hiding—uh, the fact that I—am supposed to be working, yeah! Bye!"

He took off down the street, and Mom closed the door. "Energetic," she commented with an exasperated sigh, and then turned the key in the ignition.

I settled into my seat as we pulled away, feeling an itch developing on the bottom of my foot, the one sealed off by the cast. It was a reachable tingle, nothing a good pencil eraser or chopstick couldn't handle, but the problem was, I couldn't bend over and reach it in the front seat. It began to increase its intensity, but it was nothing compared to the annoying void left by the young officer's unfinished story. I wanted to know more, sure, but I also felt bad for the guy.

Man, I thought I had it rough, I told myself.

But then, my mom said something which made me forget just how bad I felt for him and return all my pity back where it rightfully belonged: on me.

"Need to practice with those crutches when you get home, Sweetie. Tomorrow, you're going back to school."

Cue long, tragic scream: *Nooooo!* Cue clap of thunder: Boom!

And, yes, you guessed it, the massive downpour of rain.

*   *   *

It actually was storming the next day, a nice cold, wet slap in the face as I stepped out of the van to approach our town without pity's only elementary school. *Oh, boy. Let the fun begin.*

Of course, my mother had offered to walk me in, carry my backpack, wipe my nose and all the rest, but that would've been just as bad as if I had arrived only wearing a large diaper.

No, thanks. I got this, Mom.

Water running off of my raincoat like I was a giant rubber-tree plant leaf in the African rainforests, I found myself on the lower level of the school surrounded by jungle animals.

Of course, they weren't real animals, for all intents and purposes. They were children, the lower grades, and since today was Halloween, they were all dressed like their favorite four-peds. A pig bumped my bad foot and a tiger ran under my crutch like it was an open ladder.

Gotta keep moving, I told myself, even though my arms were terribly sore, and my leg was throbbing like a bass drum. I had decided to wear my army fatigues—better to show up dressed like a wounded soldier than not dressed at all and have everyone just refer to me as the wounded idiot who had fallen into a mine pit.

I was just reaching the stairs to the second story and wishing an air lift helicopter would descend, when I felt a weight lifted off my back. Shilah was beside me, dressed all in white with her chestnut hair and face all powdered white.

I was happy she was there, and that she'd grabbed my bag without asking, but the sight of her also made me mad. "Oh, really funny!" I said. "Are you supposed to be a ghost?!"

She gave me a look as we started the long, arduous journey upstairs, the first bell scattering the wildlife through the hall like the blast of a safari hunter's elephant gun. "No," she said, rolling her eyes. "I'm a giant piece of chalk."

What do you say to that?

I just suppressed a laugh and continued up, wishing someone had had the foresight to install an elevator in this place. When we got to the top, and I seriously thought I was going to drop dead, Shilah said, "You're impressive, Teddy. I would've just used the elevator."

Turns out, they had.

"Yeah," I huffed, barely able to breathe. "I don't baby this sucker—no way!" I swung myself toward the closest water fountain and practically dove into it. I gulped the cold, fresh water greedily.

"Hey, Gyros!" a passing boy said, "You're drinking from the wrong fountain, soldier!"

I looked up, water running over my lower lip. He was right. I was at the fountains by the girls' bathrooms. As a growing young man at the top of the elementary school food chain, you just didn't do that.

The rest of the day was filled with similar, heart-warming remarks.

"Watch your step, Teddy! Don't fall!"

"Maybe you should've 'mined' your own business, Gyros!"

Ha, ha, ha. Hilarious, right? Nope.

But, maybe the most troubling remark that day was the one I received, quite unexpectedly, from a teacher.

9
NOT HIM AGAIN!

It was at the end of our physical education class, the one where I hobbled around looking more like a walking protractor than anything, when Coach Peppertree, an intimidating tree-trunk of a man, dare I say, "barked" at me, "Gyros, in my office, now!"

I was clear across the gym. Kids were still milling around, blocking my path to him and his office door. *How can I possibly get there "now?" Some people are so unrealistic.*

I started my trek, using my crutches to vault over a red rubber ball rolling my way. Trying my best not to hurt too many classmates, I made it to his broom closet of an office. It was so cramped in there, his desk so small, the books, papers and trophies stacked so high everywhere, that it just made the Coach that much more hulking to look at.

I tried not to act exhausted and, fighting to balance myself in his doorway, caught sight of some odd-looking items on his desk. Normally, the guy had twisted equipment he was untwisting, or student fitness reports he was scoffing at, but not today. There was a detailed map that looked like it covered a lot of wilderness area, an aged leather journal and a book whose title I could only half make out. "An Idiot's Guide to Civil---" That was it. Was it "Civil Law," "Civil Marriages?" I didn't have time to consider all the possibilities at the moment.

"Teddy, let's not mince words!" he said in his voice that seemed to be at shouting level, even at that close of a range. "You're a wimp!"

Not a surprising comment from the world's meanest, failed-athlete-turned-gym-teacher. I was about to say, "Thank you, kindly sir, may I have another?" when he continued his non-mincing.

"I would've been off those crutches in a week or less. In fact, when I was your age—"

Oh, hang on! Here comes one of his stories!

"Well, just forget it. You gotta get to class!"

Darn! I loved a good tall tale to go with my main order of insults.

"I just wanted to remind you about the Outdoor Ed camping trip this upcoming summer. It's for the entire sixth grade. You probably didn't see the packet and permission forms I sent home, since you were piddling around, sucking your thumb."

"Um, yes, I—"

"Well, don't think you can get out of it, just because your little puny leg got a boo-boo, you got me?"

"I thought it was, um, optional?"

"Not for you, Gyros. Not if you want to make up for time lost in my class and get a passing grade."

I actually loved a good camping trip, not that I'd been on all that many, but I was particularly excited at the idea of this one.

The National Forest Service was putting it on, and they had us set on a course to learn about nature and survival, with some adventurous activities planned. So, I actually was looking forward to it. Coach Peppertree was acting so strangely, though, I decided to keep up my protests just to see if I could find out why. "I don't know. The doctors said—"

"Doctors, schmoctors!"

He was no English teacher.

"I'll tell you if and when you're ready, and you'll be ready!" He rose now to come around his desk at me. As if remembering the items there for the first time, he glanced nervously back at them and then blocked them completely from my view with his full, forest-like frame. "You reading me, Teddy boy?"

"Yes, sir," I chimed cheerily, "Just like your book on your desk about--" I tried to look around him.

"About nothing! Just make your plans and get ready. And get outta here!"

"Right, sir!" I said, over-obligingly as I spun around. Humoring his massive ego was the only way to deal with the man. I made my way out of the gym, the rubber stoppers on my crutches squeaking on the slick floor with every stilted step.

What an ending to a pretty crummy school day! I related what had happened to a pasty Shilah as we waited for my mom to pull up after school. Her powder had mostly blown away, so she looked more like an Australian aborigine now than a piece of chalk. Mom was going to take Shilah home first, since she had tuba practice (she'd made the leap from violin to the brass section weeks ago), but we knew we couldn't talk freely in the car, so I had to talk quickly.

"The best I can figure," she said in her soft voice that I couldn't in a million years imagine commanding a huge tuba, "is that he feels intimidated by you."

"What?!" I nearly choked on my after-school granola bar. "Are you talking to someone else?" I looked around.

"No, you see, people who try to put you down usually feel like they have something to prove, and it's usually about something lacking in them."

"Yeah, but Coach Peppertree!? He could sit on me with one cheek only and no one would hear from me again."

She tried to stifle a laugh as she shook her head. "It's not always about size," she said. "Look what you've done, the reputation and attention you're getting."

"You mean, freakshow loser? I could see him getting real envious over that!" I threw the rest of my snack to a bird, not feeling hungry anymore.

"Don't say that, Teddy. Everyone knows you did something special and brave for Mrs. Withers. They may not know all the details—"

"No, just that I'm crazy." Our silver taxi service rolled up the rain-slick asphalt drive, and I stood to hurriedly make my way to it. I was tired, down, and didn't feel at all like talking about myself anymore.

That's why the person waiting for me in the living room of my home was not exactly a welcome sight.

I just wanted to crash on the couch in front of the family room television and disappear into a world of flashy animation and zany sounds, but there was someone there, blocking my way.

"Hey, look who's here, Teddy," my sister Alexia said, standing just to right of our foyer in the living room, her voice a little flat. She was already in her comfy sweats, after changing out of what I liked to call her dress-to-impress school clothes, and she had a teen magazine of some sort in one hand. For the last month, this daily routine of coming right home from high school and staying there with very little outside activity was starting to concern my parents, I could tell. Her long distance relationship with boyfriend Brad from New York had failed, but in my opinion, I didn't see why this should upset her so much. She had the rest of her life to find someone much better than liver-stink Bradley.

Of course, I wasn't thinking all this at the moment. Right now, I simply wanted to collapse, and so it was with little excitement that I said, "Oh, hey Father McReedy." *Did you come to yell at me again?* I wanted to add, but didn't.

The old priest surprised me, though, with how he looked today. He wasn't the red-faced, stressed and angry man that had practically bowled Shilah and I right out of his church office in our hour of need that fateful afternoon. In fact, his hands were sheepishly holding a hat in front of him, his head was a little bowed, a slight smile on his lips, and his voice was gentle and hesitant. "Hello, Teddy," he said in his thick, Irish accent. "I know you must be tired after your first day back at school, but do you have a moment?"

He pulled out a chair for me from the dining table.

"Later!" Alexia announced her exit, and with a flap of magazine pages, she disappeared upstairs.

The front door opened behind me, and my mom entered with a dripping and fussing Leah in her arms. "But, I want it now!" she was protesting, and my mom was supplying one of her famous statements that I found myself mouthing right along with her as I moved to sit in the chair: "And who exactly told you you'd be getting everything you wanted in life?"

She noticed the old priest and leaned in for a quick side hug, "Good to see you, Father—excuse me," and she was off to the kitchen. But, not until she returned my "Did you invite him over?" look with an "I don't know why he's here!" shrug and smile.

Father McReedy sat next to me, catching one of my crutches as it threatened to slide from where I leaned it against the table. He seemed a little nervous, now, and his voice had a bit more of the rough quality that I remembered. "Well," he said. "I've come here, come to, um, apologize, lad," he told me, eyes down at first, but then connecting with mine in sincerity. "You see," he hurried on. "When you get to be my age—no, no, I shouldn't say that," he corrected himself. "The truth of the matter, son, was that I was feeling pretty low about myself at the moment you and your little friend came into my office that day. You ever feel bad about yourself?"

Still shocked at how this was going, I could only nod.

"Yeah, we all do," the pastor went on. "But, you see, mine had been going on for a little while—attendance low, bills piling up, health problems that were prohibiting me from doing what I used to be able to do. Whatever! The point is, I treated you poorly, lad, and I'm sorry."

"It's—it's okay," I said, hoping that I could move on now. Don't get me wrong. I was liking the new version of Father much better. It was just that my leg was throbbing and the couch and cartoons were sounding their siren call from the other room.

As if sensing my discomfort, McReedy stood up. "Okay, that's all," he said. "I'll see you, lad." He started for the door, but turned as he reached it. "Oh, I almost forgot. Wanted to give you --" He fished in his coat pocket and pulled something out to extend it to me in a closed fist. "Hope you'll accept this – my father gave it to me before he passed."

I leaned forward to hold out my hand. He dropped onto it a worn, silver medal on a thin chain. I turned it over to see the image of an angel bearing a sword and stepping on the head of a serpent-like figure.

"You're special, Ted," he said. "You've got a gift, but you need to know that you're not alone in the battle. I'm still trying to learn that myself after all these years, wouldn't you know? Not meant to be that way. You've got a lot of help on your side."

"Thank you, Father," I said, touched that he would give me this.

"You know," he said, "the real reason I was so grumpy that day? It was because I was angry at myself. Your courage, your passion to help Mrs. Withers, the way you believed in what you were doing. You know, it put me to shame, really. But, I want you to know, Teddy, what you've done for me since that day. You lit something in my heart that hadn't been there for a while. You gave me hope, son, hope for our world, our future—that young people could care like that, you and your friend—that you could step up and step out in faith like that—it's a hope that's growing again, Teddy, and inspiring me to do more. Like I said, I think that's how it works, how it's meant to be. You helped get me back in the game, lad, and I thank you for it."

I smiled, something growing inside of me again, something warm and real. It wasn't distinct at the moment, but it felt like a good kind of pride and purpose. I wanted to tell him how much it meant to me that he would admit this, that he would share such a personal thing with me. I didn't have the chance, though.

Father McReedy gave a nod, said, "Well, there it is. Now get better, Teddy, because we need you back in the game, too." And he was gone in the rain-washed day, just like that.

I stood there, holding the medal, thinking.

Up until that moment, I had planned on not going out that night, Halloween night-- the best candy night of the year. Why, you might ask? The leg, the crutches? With a little help, I could've surely limped to enough homes and, with the added sympathy affect I could've easily reaped quite a bounty.

The real reason was that I was afraid. Yep. Shocking, huh? But, for some reason, this year, there was something more foreboding about All Hallow's Eve to me. No doubt it had something to do with the missing librarians and all the talk of ghosts and burial grounds, but I think it had to do more specifically with my own encounter with the demon dog from nightmare-land. Almost every night, it continued to chase me in my dreams, and I wanted to make sure it didn't keep chasing me in my waking hours, too.

Yet now, holding the unexpected gift in my hand, I thought, maybe this was a sign. Maybe it's time to get out and face my fears.

Maybe, as it turns out, I picked the wrong night.

10
GHOSTS SCARE PEOPLE – BOTTOM LINE

Shilah was no longer a piece of chalk. She was a canned vegetable. Don't ask me why, but the girl showed up as a can of corn at my front door, acting as if nothing were strange at all. "Ready, Teddy?"

"Don't you look . . ." my dad started, as he leaned in to dump candy in her bag that she wasn't even holding out. With my mom out making a few quick rounds with little Bobby, the boy bunny, and Leah, girl ninja, he was on door duty, and at a loss for words.

"Corny?" Doug supplied as he came down the stairs, pulling on an overcoat. He wasn't all that happy that my parents had asked him to keep an eye on us that night. He had planned on staying at home and video chatting with his girlfriend back in Manhattan, and didn't appreciate the unscheduled delay.

I had protested heavily over the arrangement, of course. We were old enough to go out on our own, especially in this little town where everyone knew everyone. But, due to my injury, and the light drizzle outside which apparently added up to certain death for me if left unsupervised, we were all stuck with each other.

"I love your costume," I told my seventeen-year old brother while desperately trying to come up with a good zinger to defend Shilah's honor. "With your hair spiked like that, you look just like an artichoke."

"Ha, ha," he said, grabbing my neck with both of his big hands. "How's this for choking?"

"Perr-ect," I croaked. He wasn't really angry. We were just kidding around – I hoped.

He let me go with a chuckle. "Come on, G.I. Ted and Miss Corn—Wallace, is it? Let's do this."

The entire town of Witowpitee was out, it seemed, even with the rain. *Boy these people sure like Halloween*, I thought. Neighbors moved along, en masse, chatting and pushing along green goblins in strollers or herding superheroes, witches and wizards. Teen boys were zooming past wearing over-the-top gory masks, scaring girls and diving into and out of shadows. The usual.

Although, the shadows did seem to be extra dark that moonless night, and I remember a distinct feeling rising in my gut as I squeaked my way into the flow of candy-seekers: regret. What if this wasn't such a good idea?

Soon, the friendly faces and the showering of candy at a few houses, accompanied with an "Aww, Teddy, you poor thing," and a "Have an extra candy bar for your leg," made me forget that feeling. We were raking in some serious sweets and life was looking up. And then, we came to the haunted house.

This thing was incredible, with eerie lights, fog, a cemetery-like front yard and two different entrances to mazes that looked like the forbidden wings of a mysterious manor. It was at the end of a street, a cul-de-sac, and over a hundred people were milling around, waiting to go in, or just coming out.

"Let's go in!" Shilah said, struggling to fit her cylindrical body through two punk rockers. She had basically created a huge, corn-covered label and glued it to an upside-down, plastic, garbage can that had holes for her head and arms to poke through.

I couldn't help but laugh as I watched her bumping people left and right, up to the maze entrance. "Teddy, come on!" she called to me, but I was facing an even more difficult challenge, trying to get through the gathering of masqueraders without aggravating my leg.

"I'll clear a path," Doug told me, and then he dove in. "Excuse me. Can you move? Watch your tail, there," he said, as he helped me to the entrance, but not without angering a caveman and then a very tall man who wore a top hat and black cape, looking much like the famed British killer, Jack the Ripper.

What I didn't know at the time was that this latter person was Finnius Ardmyre.

"Coming in with us?" I asked Doug, who was already pulling out his cell phone to sit on a fake tombstone and broadcast how he was too mature for all this. He shook his head.

I followed my vegetative friend inside and, with a whish of his black cloak, Jack the Ripper followed me.

There was an immediate stuffed zombie that greeted you behind a cascade of cobwebs—*baby stuff*. Then, a couple of groping claws as you turned a dark corner. Shilah disappeared around this, and I was just about to, when my crutch got caught in a cauldron. I tipped it, making the dry ice pour out more mist, so much so that it choked me as I bent to fix it, breathing in the wave of carbon monoxide.

"Let me help you with that," a deep, unmistakably mortifying voice came down at me, and I realized who it was that filled the narrow passage with darkness. As he straightened up and I stumbled back around the corner, gasping for breath, the light from a strobe that reflected off of mirrored panels covering the next stretch of the maze caught his beady eyes. They were ravenous, almost elated, as he continued, "A boy in your condition can easily get hurt, Teddy Gyros. Badly hurt."

I slammed into one of the mirrors, mistaking it for the passage out.

"We're all just one misstep away from the end, you know? One wrong little turn is all it takes to find ourselves at death's door, really," he said with an odd grin, so tall that his face seemed to hover in the black void high above me, with the repetitive flashes of white making it even more horrifying than it naturally was.

"I'll take that into consideration," I managed to say, whipping my crutch out as I pushed for the next turn in the maze. Luckily, the wooden crutch hit the man's leg, and he let out a surprised "Argh!" as I jettisoned out of there.

I sped past two witches who let out their best cackles, followed by immediate, disappointed sighs as I completely ignored them, struck the wolfman at the back door in the furry foot with a rubber stopper, and then bolted out of there with the sound of his pain-filled howl in my ears.

I was in the graveyard, enshrouded in mist, and surrounded by ghostly figures, none of them Shilah, but I didn't care. I just wanted to be far, far away. So, I clambered through, vaulted over a skeleton, and hurried away down the side of the crowd, back down the street.

I hated that guy. I could honestly say. He was bad, bad to the core, and not just by accident, not just because he had a deep voice and hard features that could be mistaken as frightening. There was real evil there, no doubt, and he was going out of his way to make it known to me.

But why? What did I do to him? He's not a vampire, so what does it matter what I've done or what I do from here? I wondered these things as I widened the gap between me and the haunted house, oblivious to the fact that I was leaving my brother and my friend behind. My heart was still pounding, and I wasn't planning on stopping until it did—or at least slowed back down.

Minutes later, I was sitting on the low, decorative wall at the entrance of the next neighborhood, resting and collecting myself. I was breathing in the moist night air, when the answer hit me like a wet sock in the face.

I stood slowly, as the thoughts came together, rising up, my mouth dropping open as the dots were connected and the truth, the obvious truth that I had overlooked for so long, became clear.

Finnius Ardmyre was working for the vampires.

I know this sounds strange, but bear with me. You know those old stories of people who make pacts with evil, people who seek fame or power or money, and they think they'll get it if they join forces with the monsters that dance temptingly on the underside of reality? Beowulf, Faustus? Ever heard of these?

Well, these old stories had just made a head-on collision with my own, and there I was, standing on the side of the road, the only witness.

Red and blue lights flashed across my face, and I snapped out of my revelation daze. Beeowuup! A short siren blast sounded and I saw that it was a cop car approaching me with Officer Peters at the wheel and Shilah in the passenger seat.

"There you are!" she said. "I was worried about you. I saw that creepy mortician come out of the maze, but I didn't see you. You were gone."

"Well, Shilah," I said, "I think he's a lot creepier than you think."

"Let me give you guys a ride," Officer Peters said and, although it felt strange to be hopping into the back of a patrol car, I was glad to get off my one good foot and give my aching leg and arms a rest. What I didn't realize was that I left my candy bag on the grass when I climbed in. Yet, even later when I remembered, it hardly seemed to matter anymore, like I was finally leaving the last remnants of childhood behind.

Shilah leaned back from the front seat as we rolled forward. "You're going to explain that statement, right?"

"Wait, stop!" I shouted and the already-jumpy Peters hit the brakes hard. "What!?"

"Can you roll down the window? That's my brother over there. Need to tell him I'm with you."

And so, moments later, with an unabashedly relieved Doug on his way back home, I explained my new theory to Shilah as we rolled slowly through the gradually thinning streets.

At first Shilah gave me big eyes and then a sharp look to Officer Peters when I started to talk about our past experiences with vampires and began to tie it in to Ardmyre. But, I had already decided on one thing. Father McReedy was right. I needed to let more people help me. Shilah and I were not supposed to tackle this alone. And, since the rookie cop had let me in on his personal secret, it was time for me to let him in, too. And then hope he didn't let me right out—of his car.

"So let me get this straight," he said, still blinking in astonishment at me in the rear view mirror. "You see vampires? Because, I mean, I knew something was up—stories floating around about you, if you only knew—I just didn't know which ones to believe."

"What stories?" I asked. "Who?"

"Oh, you know, the usual small town gossip. 'Teddy's a psychic.' 'Teddy is actually an angel who helps people with their personal problems, like that old Michael Landon show.' Or, my favorite one: 'He's just like that kid who sees dead people in that Shama-lama-ding-dong movie!'"

I shook my head in amazement, looking to Shilah who just shrugged. "I didn't say anything," she assured me.

And, I knew she hadn't. My past had preceded me here, I had already suspected that, and if you combined that with the strange turn-around of Old Mrs. Withers right here in their very own town, it was natural for people to speculate.

"Hold on, Officer Peters," Shilah said, her voice low and cautious. "Where exactly are we going?"

I looked out the window. We were no longer in the neighborhoods. We were going down a dark, forested road. I felt my stomach suddenly sink.

"Oh," the young man said, his own voice shaking a little now. "We're not too far from the town square, actually. The library is just over the hill back there, and on the left, through the trees, is the open pit mine that Teddy, uh, well— you know! And, right ahead is—"

"The Walters Ranch," Shilah gasped, craning up to see the wood-carved sign at the apex of an archway of wood that framed the entrance. Walters Ranch, it read.

I closed my eyes in amazement, trying to hold back the wave of fear that suddenly reared up to swallow me whole.

"Really, Officer Peters?" I groaned. "On Halloween night?!"

"I figured, you know, what better night, right? And—and," he said, pulling the car to the right, down a capillary-like, dirt road, "I was thinking, you know, what better guy to help me investigate the ghost sightings than you, Teddy?"

I sighed. The sound of gravel protesting beneath our wheels as we eased to a stop was replaced by an overwhelming silence. Just our breathing was heard. I looked from Shilah's hesitant smirk to the young cop's entreating eyes.

"I'll make you a deal," he said, rubbing his hands together and blowing on them. It seemed to suddenly become very cold, not a trace of rain outside anymore. "I'll keep an eye on Finnius Ardmyre for you guys. You seem to think he's up to no good. In exchange, you help me take a peek around and gather enough info to write a one-page report for Captain Rogers."

This was beyond ridiculous. *Here's a good first word for your report, I wanted to say. No!*

But, somehow, against every instinct and maybe because I desperately wanted to beat the paralyzing fright that was trying to smother me, I reached for the door handle and pulled it hard.

Things couldn't have been creepier outside. The trees were behind us, wrapped with shadows that could conceal any manner of watching creature. Ahead of us was a relatively open expanse. There was a biting chill in the air and a mist rising off the grass, moisture freezing into frost.

We started walking forward, away from the car, the three of us. They were each so close on either side of me, I could barely swing my crutches out to keep moving, and I kept thinking I would knock my corn can friend over as she tottered along, and she would just roll away into the night.

It wasn't but a few minutes before we stopped, shivering in the frigid dark.

"The—the Indian burial ground is off to the right," Peters stuttered, flicking on a flashlight that barely illuminated anything. Although, I could see a large tent, probably left by the archeologists, and some dark areas in the ground where they had started digging.

He swung the light the other way. "And over there to the left, the plain slopes down into a ravine where a river runs and they take the cattle to drink."

I didn't hear any of that. I didn't even look that way, actually. Because, when the pale, white light of the flashlight was swept away, it was replaced by another pale, blue light emanating from one of the holes in the ground.

"There's nothing, right?" Officer Peters was saying. "Right, Teddy?"

I moved forward, ahead of them, to get a better view, swinging a little on my crutches. I felt Shilah grip my arm. Then, something gripped my other arm, harder, painfully harder.

It was just Officer Peters. "Ow!" I said, "Not too hard!"

"What is it?! What is it!? What is it?!" he was going into hyperventilation.

"Teddy?" Shilah asked, following my line of sight. "What is that?"

"You see it?" I breathed, more in wonder now that it came down to it, the fear subsiding almost instantly.

And then, a figure came into that light, unmistakably, an Indian man, shrouded in a moon-pale glow, although the night orb was still tucked into the clouds somewhere above us. Bare chest and legs, the loincloth at the waist, a string of feathers around his neck, it was exactly what everyone feared it would be. A tomahawk blade flashed in the light down at his side, and he was too far away for me to see his expression.

This, however, was about to change.

"O—Officer Peters?" I asked carefully, not wanting to look away, but still wanting to see if he'd seen the vision, too. Clearly, he had. He was already ten feet away from us, racing for the patrol car.

"Aaaah!" the man's scream shattered the silence, and I felt Shilah's clutching fingers dig deeper into my arm.

"Teddy!"

The ghost of the Indian was soaring toward us, raising his tomahawk, but I was too fear-struck by another dreadful apparition to fully react to this. Coming from the ravine, from the other direction, bounding through the grass at us, was the demon dog, all savage teeth and panting jowls, tearing up the earth with razor claws, bathed entirely and terrifyingly in blood-red light.

11
ANOTHER EPIC FAIL, BUT WHO'S COUNTING ANYWAY?

Here's where Teddy Gyros, yours truly, hit rock bottom. It was actually rocky bottom as, with the Indian ghost and the demon dog converging on us from both sides, I literally folded into a ball and hit the gravelly ground, leg erupting in pain as the world exploded around me. "Ah!"

My scream was suddenly wrapped in a mind-blowing mix of sounds: the roar from the beast, a shrill, other-worldly battle cry from the ghost, and then something else quite unexpected that overpowered us all—a gunshot blast!

"Hey!" was the immediate call right after the shot. "Get down!" a woman called. Then another blast. Crack!

I felt Shilah hit the ground beside me, and she started rolling, her arms and legs flailing helplessly from that ridiculous can. I reached to grab her. "Oh, no! Shilah! Shilah!"

She looked up at me, face pale, but expression angry as she tried to free herself from my hands. "I'm okay!"

Then, I noticed it. The silence again. And, sitting up, we

both saw that the Indian, the demon dog, and the lights, they were all gone.

A new figure stood over us, though, and we still had every reason to be afraid. Maybe, even more. She was a tall and strong African American, powerful-looking, like Oprah, only seventy-five percent meaner as she holstered a gun at her hip. "What in the world are you children doing out here?!" she asked, eyes fierce with incredulity. "Do you know how dangerous this place is at night? You could fall and get hurt!"

I achingly climbed to my feet and leaned on my crutches, trying to ignore the canon-fire going on inside my cast. Shilah rose beside me, and we were both speechless.

"Which officer is that, back there, hiding underneath his car?"

Shilah looked at me. The truth would come out eventually. It was just a matter of which version to choose right now.

The woman sighed, her face softening—by one brow-crease. "I'm Agent Lorna Wood," she said, flashing what looked like an FBI badge in the dark. "I'm in charge of the investigation into the missing librarians, was here discussing some finer points with Mr. Walters up at his house when we saw your car come this way."

A man on a muscular, tan and white mare became visible, riding back from the direction of the burial ground area. Bushy mustache and beard, cowboy hat sitting far back so his frock of grey hair was showing beneath it, it was Mr. Tom Walters. "Nothing," he reported to the woman.

"So you did see what we saw!?" I blurted out.

"There's nothing under here, either!" came the voice of Officer Peters who jumped out from under his car. He was all teeth, sheepishly smiling as he brushed off his uniform. "Yep, all clear!"

Shilah winced a little in embarrassment.

Agent Wood gave him a look and then glared squarely at me. "No, young man, I didn't see anything."

But, you fired your gun! I wanted to challenge her. Yet, I was afraid to say anything. I didn't have to.

"I fired my gun," the woman supplied, "because the two of you looked so incredibly frightened, I thought it would snap you out of whatever trance you were in." Her hard stare made her words convincing enough, but I couldn't help wonder if she was telling the truth. "Excuse me a moment," she said, and then pulled Officer Peters aside.

What followed was a very intense "talking-to" that she gave to the poor, young rookie, and I couldn't catch all of it, but was certain I heard things like, "Suspend your badge in a heartbeat," and "Have you cleaning toilets for the rest of your life!" And, these seemed like the nicest things she was saying.

During the middle of her torrent of chastisements, Walters reined his horse over to us. "Little lady," he acknowledged Shilah with the tip of hat, and then he said to me, "What's your name, son?"

"Ted. Teddy Gyros, sir."

"Yeah, I figured as much." He glanced over at the agent and then, with his deep, rumbling voice hushed, he said, "Between you and me, there is something terrible going on here. That lovely woman over there may have read too many scholarly books in her days to believe it, so, I guess what I'm sayin' is, you and your friends are welcome back here any time."

I couldn't believe my ears, but tried to play it cool. I was still shaking all over like the last leaf of Fall. "Roger that, sir." I nodded in false confidence, cringing inside at how stupid that sounded. *'Roger that?!' Where did that come from?!*

He went on. "My men and I have scoured this place over and over, without seeing nothing or finding nothing. These things hide when they want to and come out when it suits their purposes. You seem to suit their purposes, Teddy. So, in case you don't catch my meaning, I'm saying this whole thing may right well be up to you."

I didn't know what to say. Had he or had he not just witnessed my cowardly display of ground-hugging? I didn't have a chance to say anything. Agent Angry Woman was back in front of us.

"I want you two to get back in that car with the soon-to-be demoted officer, and go back home, and don't even give a shredded wheat of a thought about coming back here—Let the professionals handle this from now on, you understand me?"

Who could escape her gut-grinding glare? How could we each say anything except, with tails tucked firmly between our legs, "Yes, Ma'am."

* * *

Needless to say, I didn't sleep well that night. Or, for the next seven nights, for that matter. It was all too much for me. Even though Shilah and I had tried our best to work it through, munching on the Halloween treasures she so graciously shared with me (thankfully, she was still unwilling to leave her childhood completely behind). I still couldn't put it all together, couldn't get a firm foothold to climb on top of it and come up for air. I felt like I was drowning in a sea of swirling feelings, facts and freakish fiction.

Two things, at least, I was confident of: one, was my painful lack of confidence. It wasn't just a lack, let me tell you. It was as if someone had taken whatever confidence I had hoped to hold onto since my injury, grounded it into a fine powder, mixed it with instant fruit punch mix and then drank the whole thing down in front of me while I looked on, helpless and disgusted.

I was disgusted at myself, really. I couldn't understand it. What was wrong with me? I kept playing the events of Halloween night over and over in my mind, and couldn't escape the fact that I had failed miserably, had let everyone down, most importantly Shilah. What if Agent Wood hadn't shown up? What if those creatures had gotten to her?

It would've all been my fault, again! I was completely useless in defending her, in doing anything really.

The second wonderful conclusion we were able to pull out of all this by a very thin thread, was that the disappearance of the librarian, Miss Lucy, and possibly the first one, Ms. Crumberly, was tied directly to the strange sightings at the Indian burial ground.

There didn't seem to be any coincidence that these things were happening at once. We even traced back the original discovery of the Indian Burial ground to around the same time the first librarian had vanished.

It seemed to me that the Indian ghost was a vampire posing as a ghost who, along with his precocious pet, Fang-face, was trying to scare people away from that area. Naturally, people would assume that it was just because the burial ground had been disturbed. You dig up Indian bones, you get angry, Indian ghosts. Logical conclusion.

And this was what the vampire wanted us to believe. However, Shilah and I knew there was something more to it. The biggest question that needed to be answered was Why? Why kidnap these ladies? What did he have to gain, other than the satisfaction of the pure evil of it all? And, even if it was simply that, would the librarians be found at the burial ground if only people would dig deeper?

"They can't do any more digging there," Shilah had said, "until the FBI works things out with Walters." So we were at a standstill in that department, until more information could be unearthed, literally.

Last, but certainly not least on the growing list of mysteries was Finnius Ardmyre. What exactly was his involvement in all this? Was he so threatening toward me because he knew that, if I could defeat one vampire, like I had in Old Mrs. Withers' basement, I could do the same to more? But, I was just one kid. There were literally thousands of them, if not more in this little town alone, I was sure. So, how much harm could I really do in their grand, evil scheme of things?

True to his word, Officer Peters tried his best to keep an extra eye on the town's tallest creep-o. But, due to his new station in life, he had very little freedom during the day to do so.

Because, also true to the FBI Agent's word, Officer Peters had been immediately demoted from patrolman to traffic beat cop the next day. And, in a town with very little traffic to direct, this was quite the humiliating setback.

So, it was with very little movement on all fronts that one week, and then two weeks painstakingly passed. I thought for sure that Agent Wood would make some sort of breakthrough, or we'd get some report, clue or revelation from Officer Peters.

One thing was for certain. I wasn't getting involved anymore. I would follow the path of my sister Alexia: go to school, head home right after with my head low, and then stay there. That's about all I was good for.

Shilah, of course, had volunteered to do some snooping

around, herself, but I pleaded with her not to. The words of the FBI agent seemed to ring continually in my ears: *Let the professionals handle it.*

She was right. Of course she was. It was stupid of me to think that I had to be the one to save the day. Stupid pride.

Yet, at the end of two weeks, on the day I had labeled Freedom Day, when I was set to finally have my cast removed, something changed my attitude almost completely.

It was a voice, a strange and unexpected one, and it was coming from my older sister's room.

12
TIME TO GET ON YOUR HORSE, SON

The morning had been a glorious one, filled with chocolate chip celebratory pancakes and chirping birds fluttering and bringing life to the leafless and skeletal-looking tree in our front yard.

"Freedom!" I shouted as I hobbled outside after my mother, the cry scattering the birds. They went into a wonderful arch in the crisp, blue sky, in perfect formation, and then returned back to their favorite tree, resuming their roles as living leaves.

A half an hour later, a satisfying Crack! A long slit down the cast by Dr. Phillips, and I experienced one of the greatest feelings of relief in my short life. I was free.

It was almost like my leg itself took a giant, deep breath and exhaled in tearful, speechless joy. But, when I looked down at it, I noticed just how small and weak it looked in comparison to my other leg.

"That's normal!" the doctor said, along with "Keep up the physical therapy, kid, and you'll be back to normal in no time!"

But, it was with a lot less enthusiasm that I returned to the house later that morning, the birds quiet, as if sensing my mood-- or bracing themselves for another outburst. I gingerly made my way up the front porch steps, clinging to the rail.

Tired of having to wait and bide my time any longer, I had wanted to do this without the crutches, my leg still tender and sore, but functional.

"I can do it!" I said, in answer to my mom's offer of help. But then, after two steps, I fell onto the porch rail. "Just-- not right now."

My mom rushed up to hand me my crutches. "No big deal, Teddy. Give it a little more time, okay, tiger?"

I wanted to roar out in frustration at this, but my mom, and the birds had heard enough of me lately. I sulked towards my room, taking the steps one stinking, wooden reminder of my stupidity at a time. Thirty-seven rectangular placards that announced with each step, "Nice going, Gyros." "Who were you kidding, anyway?" "You brought this all on yourself."

It was at step twenty-eight, though, that the strangest thing happened. I heard, coming from Alexia's slightly open door to her room, the voice of Gary Greystone, the library manager. Of course, I thought as I paused there, she's watching one of his news interviews online!

Alexia had a laptop that she often used in her room for homework or entertainment. I didn't know why she would want to watch that plaster-faced—

But then, I heard the words, "Of course, Alexia. You would be great, darling! Don't undersell yourself."

Whoah. Wait a minute, here.

I stepped closer to the door to look inside. Sure enough, there was that slick, chiseled face on Alexia's laptop on her desk. She had her back to the door, facing the computer and video chat session. She flipped her hair to one side, something I saw her do often, when she was—wait, hold on! Flirting?!

"Gary, you're so sweet! I really could use the extra money, that's for sure. And, if you think I can meet the requirements—"

"Well, I'd like to meet and go over them with you, if that's all right with you, Alexia."

"Yes! I'm totally free today! I ditched school, told my parents I had the flu. Really, I was just hoping to talk to you again."

This was all too much for me. I wanted to throw up right into her room. How could she--?! The guy was a scumball, obviously. He had done zero to help find the missing librarians, and more to help his own celebrity status in the last two months, and anyone with half a brain--

"Okay," I heard my sister say, with a little clap of her hands. "I'll meet you at the library at five, then! Bye!"

"Until then, darling," he smiled, his teeth nearly glowing white, and then he was gone.

Alexia jumped up and ran for her door in bubbly excitement.

There was nothing I could do but back up as she swung her door open and stopped in her tracks. I knew she was going to lay into me something fierce for eavesdropping. I braced myself.

"Oh, hi Teddy!" she said, leaning in to kiss me on the cheek. "You got your cast off! Yeah! I'm so happy for you!" And she started down the steps.

I was too shocked for a moment, and she almost got away,

before, "Alexy, wait!"

She stopped her descent, a wide grin on her face. "What, Ted?"

I hadn't seen her so happy in weeks. I faltered, tried to find the right words. I hated to burst her newly blown bubble, but something rose up inside of me, a burning sensation all of a sudden. I was her brother, and I had to say something. "Don't go!" was all I could say at first.

"Wh-what?"

"To meet that guy, Greystone."

"Teddy, were you listening--?"

"Listen to me!" I nearly shouted. For some reason, this meant a lot to me all of a sudden. "Listen, he's—he's worse than Bradley."

"This is for a job!"

"Oh, right! I saw how you guys—and why would you want to work at that place anyway, when the last two--?"

"It's to be his secretary, okay? To help him type out his memoirs, not to be a librarian."

"Oh, I don't believe this!"

"And I don't have to listen to you and your—"

"No, you do! He's a phony, okay? He acts like he cares, but can't you tell? He doesn't!"

The joy was starting to drain from her face like the pieces of candy that shoot out of those twenty-five cent dispensers too fast and scatter everywhere. "You don't—know him. You've only seen him on TV," she told me, pointedly.

"But, I have a feeling--!"

"Oh, of course! One of your feelings. One of Teddy's famous, foolproof feelings!"

This hurt me. I thought about turning and bolting at that moment. She seemed to sense this and so she didn't move either. I shook my head.

She seemed sorry. "Teddy, I--"

"No, it's okay," I said. "I get that. I deserve it, too. But, it's not like that at all, Sis. I just want you to know that I think—I think you deserve a whole lot better than him. That's all. A million times better."

I didn't even look her in the eye after this, didn't even know if my words had hit home. I just turned and continued my groaning journey upwards. All I knew was that, after five minutes of sitting on my bed and staring at the door, she didn't follow me. She didn't come.

Which meant, unfortunately, that she was going, going to the library.

Someone else showed up at my door, just as I was about to dive back into my bed and pull the covers over my head for about a month.

It was my dad.

"Hey, Ted," he stood in the doorway, in his work clothes. At this time of the day, that meant only one thing. My mom had called him and he had made a special trip home, for me.

Here it comes, I thought, rubbing my scrawny leg, feeling as weak and small as it looked. More lecturing.

"Look," he said, hands in his pockets. "I don't know exactly how to process all this myself. It's not in the parenting books. I know you are special, no doubt in my mind. But, what does that mean? What are we supposed to do with it, right now, at this point in your life?"

He paced a little. I was all ears. I'd never heard him even come close to acknowledging the "special gift" that seemed more like a curse, the thing that had he and my mother so worried, that had prompted the move from New York.

"All I know is that you're my son, my life, and I couldn't

bear to see you hurt," he said, squatting down in front of me now, touching my knee. "That's why I said what I said back at the hospital. I'm sorry, I really am, but I was trying—I was trying to just get you to stop, stop putting yourself in harm's way out of some misguided sense of—of I don't know what." He dropped down to a knee with a sigh, looking at my porthole window that was closed, shutter drawn. "But, Teddy, there's something worse than physical harm, and I think you and I have both seen that now."

"I—have?" was all I could say, though I knew what he was referring to. I was just too ashamed to admit it.

He nodded. "It's deep inside you, a dying deep in there, when you look inside and you can't see anything good anymore, you don't see anything worthwhile or-- or important. I think it's my fault, you know? You see me get down sometimes because of my career not going well, or the bills not getting paid like they should. I get a rejection or a bad review at work, and I let it get to me. Maybe I haven't shown you well enough that none of that matters."

He lifted my chin to look right into my eyes with his own, the ones that seemed to always understand me better than anyone else.

"This is very important. Who we are, who you are, Teddy—your value in this world, it has nothing to do with how many times you succeed and how many times you fail. You got that? We are all going to fail, sometimes a lot. Babe Ruth struck out just as many times as he hit all those home runs. But, he kept swinging, you know?"

I knew that already. He had told me that during Little League as a kid, but it was good to be reminded again.

"Try to see yourself as I see you," my dad said. "You're this amazing kid, and not because of what other people think of you or because of anything you've done, actually, but simply because you are you. You're my son."

I had to look away. I really didn't want to cry, not right now.

My dad stood and crossed to open the shutters of my window, letting the light in. "Then," he said, "you step up to home plate, you lift your chin, and you give it your all, okay? And, whatever happens, you at least know you did your best. That's all we're asked to do. Just give it all we've got. And if we go down, well, we go down swinging, right? But, what we usually find out is, when we do our best, even if it's not perfect, even if we think we've failed, help comes to us and things usually turn out better than we could have imagined."

He gave me one of his famous hair rustles, searching my eyes with his "Am I getting through to you?" look. I gave him a little nod. He had gotten through.

"All right," he said, putting a small slip of paper down on the bed next to me before turning for the door. "Father McReedy dropped that by my work. He said it goes with the gift he gave you last time. See you tonight at dinner, son."

I wanted to say "Thanks, Dad," but there was so much emotion welled up in my throat, I was afraid any sound I let escape would just open the floodgates of emotion. He seemed to sense this, gave me a wink, and left.

I turned the paper over. For the longest time I stared at it, the words blurring after a moment as new thoughts fired in my mind like sparks igniting cylinders that were more than anxious to get going again.

Yes, it was time to get going. This much was unmistakably clear now.

No one else had been called to this juncture in time. No one else could stop my sister from another big, heartbreak-mistake or help find those missing women like I could, really, when it came down to it. And it was not because I was this incredible guy, this superstar. No, it was simply because I was who I was.

And, I had learned another important thing: I was still just one part of all this. It wasn't entirely up to me and what I thought I was or wasn't capable of doing. There was a great deal of help on my side, and I needed it, relied on it now to get me through.

Yes, it was time to go back to the library. But, not alone.

13
BACK IN THE BATTLE

Have you ever tried to ride a bike with one leg? It's awkward. You inevitably hit your shin or scrape the back of the leg you're trying not to use with the metal of the pedal you're trying not to push.

"Ooh—Ahh!" I got a nice double blow as I coasted out of my neighborhood, trying not to use my sore leg as much as I normally would.

The sun was putting its bathing cap on, getting ready to dive into the dark sea of night, but not quite yet. It was four-thirty. I had just enough time to meet Shilah at her house and then head to the library together, where Officer Peters would later join us on his way home from his less-than-glorious beat. I had to hand it to Shilah. She'd done a superb job of convincing him to get out and face it all again, to regain his honor, and to make it up to two kids he had left in the line of fire on Halloween night. Cheap tactic, yes, but it worked.

So, we were the new vampire-fighting trio. What more help could I draw on?

The answer bobbed against my chest a little, cool and reassuring against my skin. It was the medal from Father. And, the words from the prayer card that went with it rang out in my ears now, as it did back at home while I packed the backpack now snuggly strapped to me.

Saint Michael the Archangel, defend us in battle…

Cross-stake, sharp and ready, inside the backpack.

Be our safeguard against the wickedness and snares of the devil…

Walkie-talkies for Shilah and I. Holy water bottles, enough for all three of us—check!

May God rebuke him we humbly pray…

And finally, the medal of one of the most powerful angels, placed slowly around my neck.

And do thou, O Prince of the Heavenly Host, cast into hell Satan and all the evil spirits who prowl about the world, seeking the ruin of souls.

The last words rang in my ears again as I pulled up to Shilah's house. She was waiting outside, holding the handlebars of her own ten-speed. With a nod, she jumped on and started pedaling right alongside of me.

Amen.

There was no time for discussion. No time whatsoever to waste.

We rode hard and fast, me kicking back in with my recovering leg, fighting the pain. As we made our way to the center of town, the air cold but still dry like the streets and sidewalks, I went over in my mind the plan we had discussed and agreed upon earlier.

Alexia was our first objective. If she wouldn't listen to me, maybe she'd listen to another girl. Granted, Shilah was four years younger than her, but still, it was worth a shot. We were hoping to be able to convince her to call off the interview/date with Glue-Hair Gary before it could even start. All she had to do was walk away.

Then, we would make our next move. Shilah and I were certain that the tunnel beneath the shed near the library played a part in all this, and that we could figure it out together. While we did this, Officer Peters would station himself in the trees near the Indian burial ground and communicate to us by walkie-talkie if he caught sight of the vampire on the move.

Things were bound to get scary. It was going to get rough, a lot go wrong, maybe, but I felt a renewed sense of peace come over me as I passed the Civil War soldier frozen in the town square. I saluted him, tried to remind myself to get the story from Shilah about that guy when this was all over, and then proceeded to the side of the library where we stashed our bikes.

I couldn't help but grin to myself as I watched this girl hero stride confidently up the steps of the library and push through the big double doors as she had done on our first adventure together. She never broke stride. She was constant and confident through all of this, the real hero in my eyes.

Was it just coincidence that we had moved to this town at this time in my life to find someone here who clicked so well, who stepped so well right in stride with me? No, I didn't think so. This was meant to be.

Two minutes later, she was frowning at me outside a tiny administrative office. "Well, Teddy, that part just wasn't meant to be right now. We'll catch up to her later, I'm sure."

I shook my head. I was really worried about Alexia, more than ever for some reason, and what the assistant library manager had told us was cause for greater concern. "He's such a sweetie," she'd said, a mid-fifties woman who talked just like a teenager about her boss. "He decided the library was too stuffy for an interview with your sister, so he left early to meet her for ice cream. Isn't that precious?"

I had wanted to use the sanitizing wipes on the woman's desk to wipe her adoring smile off her face, but I somehow managed to restrain myself.

Now, as we passed back into the main library, open once more to the public, though hardly full like it had been in the past, I saw through a side window, the sun dipping in for its night swim. We only had a half hour or so before the light was totally gone. So, there was no way to go and find my sister and make it back in time. "Let's go," I told Shilah, adjusting my backpack.

"Out the back?"

"Sure," I said, less than enthusiastically. I was starting to feel that sick feeling inside. Already, part one of our plan was off track.

It was about to get a whole lot worse.

We walked out the back door and, breathing in the dusk, I tried to clear my mind. There was a grassy area where some children were playing and a couple of adults were sitting, reading books. They had no idea what was going on, and part of me envied them.

Would my life be better if I just forgot about what happened in New York, with Mrs. Withers and ignored the things I couldn't help but see?

My father's words came back to me at that moment, and it steeled my resolve. This was who I was. And, besides, I had to stop thinking that this was all, somehow, just about me. There was so much more at stake here.

"Teddy," Shilah got my attention, indicating her watch. It

was ten minutes past five.

We hurried down a side trail that led to the forest, back to the place where this new, dark chapter of my life had started. Maybe my right leg sensed we were getting near and it was trying to slow me down, stop me, but it hurt to no end at the moment, and I had to limp heavily, put most of my weight on my other one. I reached for the rough bark of the first pine and leaned on it heavily, then pushed on.

Under the deeper cover of the trees, we stopped and Shilah pulled out the walkie-talkies from my backpack.

"Officer Peters, do you read me?" she asked into hers.

Static. No reply. She looked to my face, my frustration mounting.

"Officer Peters, are you there?"

More white noise.

"Well," I started to say, thinking we should call the entire thing off if our back-up wasn't in place, when—

"Yes, Shilah, I read you," the voice of the young police officer came back through the tiny, black device in her hand. "I'm in position now. Sorry. Had to go to the bathroom."

We couldn't help but laugh.

I lifted my walkie-talkie to my mouth and squeezed the button. "Any sign of the you-know-what's?" I asked. We had to speak in code in case anyone else was listening in on our channel.

"That's a negatory, Big Apple," he said, and, hearing it now, I really didn't like the code name he'd given me.

"Copy that, Pan-Cake. We're moving in," I said. Maybe it was a combo reference to his childhood hero and his favorite breakfast food, but it didn't exactly instill much confidence in me at the moment.

We headed toward the shed.

In the waning daylight, it was a lot less creepy than the night I first encountered the demon dog who almost drove me to an early grave. I tried to breathe, tried to look brave for Shilah's benefit, though she seemed unshaken.

"He's just down there," she pointed to our right, and I realized, if the trees weren't there, we'd see the Indian burial ground on that side, down at the bottom of the huge hill we were descending at the edge of the Walters Ranch. On the opposite side, I hated to even think of it, was the open pit mine.

We passed the shed, and I admit, a huge part of me was glad we hadn't planned on going inside the wood-paneled place of terror. No, we were following up on a hunch that Shilah had, something that she remembered from the night we got separated and she had scoped out the area.

"I remember the ground felt weird in one spot," is what she'd told me, a while back, "like it was hollow in one place." Now, we were going to check it out, hoping we'd find something the police and FBI had missed.

If the tunnel beneath the shed was sealed off, was a dead end, then there was no reason why it couldn't continue on the other side of this blockage, and maybe that hollow spot on the ground was the opening to it.

We came to the area past the shed that had a few trees clumped by a path which connected to the one running back up the hill to the library grounds. The soft earth was covered in pine needles, a thick layer, dry and crackling under our feet.

Shilah began shuffling around, sweeping some aside. "No, that's not it." She stepped over to her left. "Closer to here, I think." And she ran her foot through the pine needles, bunching them up like a human rake. But, there was nothing but dirt there, too.

I stepped toward her, and then my heart skipped a beat. The sound my good foot had made was not exactly what it should've been. It was like it had hit—

"Uh, Shilah," I called to her. Then, I looked down, scooping aside the dry, pointy greenery and revealing, directly beneath me, a square, wooden plank.

She rushed to me and quickly cleared it off more. It had hinges on one end and a handle on top at the other. It was just what we had thought, another entrance to another part of the tunnel. Shilah's eyes met mine.

This was huge.

And, the next logical step would've been to open the latch and continue the exploration. This was what I would've done two months ago, easily. But, if there was one thing my injury had taught me, it was patience.

Okay, maybe I was still working on patience! The real thing I'd learned was to listen to the gal that stood beside me now.

"Let's cover it back up," she said, and we worked together to do so.

Then, we moved into our next position to wait. Surveillance: It wasn't glamorous or adventurous, but it was exactly what was needed now. We would wait in the cover of the woods and the encroaching night, wait as long as we needed to until someone showed up to use that hatch. Then, we'd call Officer Peters, and he'd bring the law down on this dastardly person.

We settled into a good spot behind some bushes between two trees, and I couldn't help think, as the shadows began to melt together, it would more likely be some-thing that showed up, something with claws, savage teeth and lots of drool.

14
DANGERS IN THE DARK

The time passed like a stick through mud. Maybe not that slow, but it's what it felt like, and it wasn't just because the bottom of my jeans was getting wet with mud from yesterday's rain.

Officer Peter's voice came to us low and quiet over my walkie-talkie as we sat, Shilah and I, watching the area behind the shed. We strained our eyes to make sure we didn't miss anything in the moon-blotched night that only gave patches of light here and there through the dense tree-tops.

"Do you ever feel like you're not alone when you're alone?" he was asking us, perched in a very similar position in the lip of woods near the Indian burial ground.

"Yeh," I said, exchanging a look with Shilah.

"That's how I feel sometimes," the young cop told us. "You know, my sister, she did get better, Teddy, like I told you. But only for a while. Only a year. Then, she—she was gone. Gone, but not really, you know? I feel like she's still here.

It's the only way I've made it this far as a police officer. Every time I get afraid, afraid of my shadow, I think I can hear her voice telling me, 'You can do it. You can do it.'"

I could tell by Shilah's inquisitive look that she was lost. I hadn't told her anything about my encounter or talks with Officer Peters. It wasn't my story to tell. It was his.

"Do you know why she says that, Teddy?" his voice asked in the dark.

I pressed the button to reply. "Why?"

"Because, before she died I told her about the deal I had made with the gypsy lady, told her how scared I was that my shadow was now, well, a shadow of death."

I felt Shilah's hand grip my leg. I gave her a little nod.

"We all have to die, I know. It's just part of life, I keep telling myself. But, I just want to do it right, you know, not afraid, not like a coward. 'You can do it, Hunt.' She called me that, short for Hunter. 'It's not as bad as you think,' she told me. 'It's actually much better, Hunter. You can do it.'"

There was static now, silence for a long, long moment. Neither of us wanted to make a sound or a move.

Then, my walkie-talkie clicked and his voice was back. "The problem is, Teddy, I don't believe her."

Three things happened now, at pretty much the same moment. The first was the form of the Indian ghost coming out of the burial ground and soaring right towards Officer Peter's position. "Oh- Oh!" he stuttered over the radio. "It's coming!"

This first thing distracted us from the second thing, the figure approaching Shilah and me from behind. We were too busy trying to get answers from Peters.

"What? What's coming?"

Silence.

"Officer Peters?"

More silence, then, through the static, the sound of faltering breath and, "The ghost!"

Shilah looked at me, but quickly jolted back, as the figure loomed over my back.

"I'll take those now," the deep, nearly emotionless voice announced who it was, and I turned to see our unfriendly neighborhood mortician standing like a fire-charred, lifeless tree over me. "The radios—hand them here, both of you." His demand was punctuated now with both impatience and the revolver that nearly blended in with his large, black-gloved hand.

Surprisingly, I wasn't too afraid of the man anymore, even armed as he was now. No, I saved most of my horror for the third thing, the creature that stood at his feet, its fierce eyes and teeth baring right at me: the demon dog.

This is not good.

We stood together, still gripping our walkie-talkies out of fear, paralyzing fear, I'm sure. By the way Shilah was trembling and staring down at the man's legs, I knew she could see the hound of hell, too.

"I won't ask you a third time," Finnius Ardmyre told us. "My little friend here gets quite hungry this time of night."

There was nothing we could do but throw the hand-helds down.

"Teddy?" Officer Peter's voice came crackling through. "Shilah! He's—he's headed your way!"

Ardmyre stepped on one walkie-talkie—Crunch! Just like those poor snails! Then, the other. It gave a last dying whisper of white noise and then, it went silent.

At this moment, as if the dog was sensing either the officer or its approaching master, it lifted its nose, let out a short, chilling howl, and then bounded off through the trees down the hill in the direction of the Indian burial ground. It left a trail of streaming red light behind it.

"Move along now, Teddy Gyros— fifty-eight inches tall, twenty-four wide; Shilah Pearson—fifty-six inches tall, eighteen wide." He was listing our coffin sizes; a frightening touch from a man who didn't really need to prove his point any further. He was evil and mean to children, too. Not a good combo.

He led us to the back of the library shack and right to the spot where we'd discovered the hatch earlier. With one swipe of his black, innocence-crushing boot, the man cleared off the pine needles. "Open it, Mr. Gyros," he commanded me.

I tried desperately to fight the fingers of fear crawling all over my body, working their way up to my throat to cut off the air to my brain. Breathe! I told myself. Keep your head clear!

Shilah helped me, her calm, steady look reassuring me, and we opened the large hatch with a heave and a resulting Thud! The top of a wooden ladder was all that was visible, the rest of it disappearing into the gaping hole in the earth below.

"Well, we should be going now," I told the man, switching to my cheery, humor-the-gym-coach tactic. "If there's anything else we can do to help you, Mr. Ardmyre, just let us know!"

"Climb inside, both of you," he said, with a slight, cautious glance around.

"We have flashlights in our backpack, sir," Shilah spoke up now, mimicking my tone nicely. "It's awfully dark down there. If you don't mind, I can get those." And she started to unzip the pack on my back.

"Never mind that! Just move," he said, clearly rattled by how un-rattled we were now acting.

It was a good try by Shilah. The flashlights could've

attracted some much-needed outside attention. But at least she had managed, I found out later, to slip an item out that would come in quite handy later.

I gave one last look to the trees, hoping to see Officer Peters come charging through at any moment, but there was nothing.

I went first and, the girl following quickly after, we descended into the black. The ladder creaked with every rung we clung to, but it was strong and held us to the end. At the bottom, the air was dust-filled, but cool, not stifling like the other tunnel had been; the one on the other side of us where I'd first met the pernicious pooch. This one was a lot bigger, I could tell, even in the dark.

I was sure Shilah was thinking the same thing as me while the bad man filled the gap in the roof above us, closing the hatch and plunging us in complete darkness: we could run, make a break for it with the flashlights lighting our way and hopefully—

Sizzle-Crack! It was the sound of a very old switch snapping on and completing a circuit of electricity, and with a brief flicker, a string of old, wire-covered lights along the beams bracing the earth above our heads came to life. It lit the tunnel that stretched on for a good fifty feet, just as I'd suspected.

It also revealed the gun that our archenemy Ardmyre kept pointed at us, skillfully, as he worked his way down the ladder. "There! That's better, isn't it?" He seemed relieved that we were out of sight and alone, where no one else could see us or hear our screams for help.

So, this is where he's taken the librarians, I thought to myself, as he motioned for us to move. We preceded him down the passage. *But why take us, now?* What on earth could he possibly be thinking? Why add the charges of kidnapping two children onto the charges of abducting two adults? It was stupefying to me.

But, I learned a valuable lesson that night, and it wasn't simply that evil makes people do stupid things. It was that this man, his eyes lit by the same glow that had lit the wide-eyes of gold-seekers nearly a century ago, really believed in what he was doing, and passionately, too. He was convinced, wholeheartedly that his dark, sinister plan was the right, normal and foolproof one. And, how did I find this out, you might wonder?

Because, he told me.

15
DARKER PLANS COME TO LIGHT

"I know it's a bit cliché for me to start telling you this," the man said as we came to a fork in the passage. "Stay to the left," his low voice commanded.

Shilah and I veered left, walking slowly, almost too slowly. We were in no rush to get to the end of the line, that's for sure.

"But, you know, now that I've come to it, I understand why, in the books or in the movies, the villain does this. It's simply irresistible. Here, at my moment of triumph, with no plausible way of you surviving the night—"

This shot a chill through my bones that I fought to ignore.

"—I find it extremely satisfying to let you know just how smart I've been and just how miserably you've failed."

I'm not a failure, not a failure, I told myself, over and over. *He's just trying to disarm me from the inside out.*

"You see, we anticipated this, foresaw you coming here, delivering yourselves right into our grasp."

"So, you're not alone?" I said.

"Of course not. There are so many more of us than you think, boy. Go right," he ordered.

We took a passage that branched off to the right from the main one. Twisting and turning this way and that, this tunnel was definitely more freshly dug. And, by the looks of the lights connected to the rafters above, a Home Depot special had been taken advantage of. This was a new shaft, and it ran in the direction of the Indian burial ground. Clearly, Ardmyre and company were digging for something. The question was, what did it have to do with me?

As if sensing my questions, he supplied the answers. "Wonderful work, isn't it?" his pointed rat teeth flashed a proud smile that was revolting to see. "Not bad for being done by women, eh?"

Shilah looked at me. *The librarians!*

"Yes, yes, the librarians, of course," he said. "You didn't expect me to do all the digging myself, did you? Or any of it!" the man boomed. "I have a business to run, you know. And they were so helpful at researching and pinpointing exactly where we should dig, helping us avoid hindering underground caverns and rock deposits that had been documented by geologists years ago-- such a valuable contribution to the effort."

"Which is?" I asked, as we came to a doorway on the right of the passageway that continued on further.

Finnius Ardmyre pulled a ring of keys from his pocket. There must have been nearly thirty keys on there, and, as he fit the one to the lock on this door, my stomach cringed at the thought of what horrors the other ones led to as well.

"Fitting that you should ask the question, Mr. Gyros," he said, as he unlocked the door and rested a murderous glove on the knob. "Since you, it seems, are the answer. All along, we've been digging down here for what we were told was an element of power buried deep within our little town of Witowpitee. Such a great power that my masters wished me to stop at nothing to find it-- find it, they said, and destroy it."

"Why destroy it?" Shilah asked, sliding her hand out of her coat pocket to rest on her hip.

The tower-like man let out a terrible laugh that ran up and down the mine shaft and our spines. He was nearly perpendicular due to the low roof, his face protruding down at us, and we could see in his crazed eyes just how lost in his own delusions he was. But he was not the only one, we would find out.

"Wouldn't you know," he said, seemingly ignoring my friend's question, "that it turned out the power was buried deep within you, Teddy," he sneered at me. I never hated the sound of my childhood nickname more than when it rolled off his serpentine tongue. "A boy. A small, insignificant boy. I was never more surprised and, to tell you the truth, I've been fighting the reality of it all for weeks, now. But, my masters know best, and must be unwaveringly obeyed."

Power!? What power? Is it my second-sight, the ability to detect the evils like vampires and their house-pets around me? Was that really something his 'masters' were so afraid of? My mind reeled. He was right. I was just a boy; one boy at that.

Thankfully, Shilah prodded him with more questions, while I tried to rein in my thoughts. "These masters told you to kidnap the librarians, then, is that why you did it, Mr. Ardmyre? Voices, strange spirits told you?"

"Who said anything about strange spirits?!" he shouted,

face clouding with a flash of anger that passed into a sickening look of adoration. "They are the immortal ones, the beautiful ones!"

"And they promised to make you just like them?" she asked, her voice so clearly unafraid, her eyes so purely shining he regarded her almost like she was some sort of alien flower.

"What they promised me, little girl, is none of your concern," he said, slowly. "You should be more concerned with your poor choice in friends, Miss Pearson." He opened the door at this point, a strange smell hitting us, but nothing more, just darkness, a void that his echoing voice filled eerily. "And it shall be reported hereafter, that you and your friend, Mr. Gyros, poor and misguided youths as you were, went searching for the lost librarians, and what you found was most horribly unexpected—"

He motioned us at gunpoint inside the door and we had no choice but to comply. We stepped inside, turning to face him.

"—a tragedy really, the one that ended your short, meaningless lives. The tunnels, you see, are so unstable; one little tremor and the whole network will come right down. They were, I told you, built by women after all." He slammed the door shut on us at that moment and we heard the key turn the lock once more, sealing us in.

His cold-hearted voice was still loud enough to reach us through the door. "And so, as the masters once prophesied, the element of power becomes buried indeed, buried beneath our little town of Witowpitee, forever."

I half-expected to hear his maniacal laugh reverberating off the tunnel walls as he walked away in triumph, but maybe he suppressed that. Maybe that would've been too cliché.

What we did hear turned out to be something even more bone-chilling, more unsettling: the whispers in the dark.

16
A TRIPLE THREAT

There was a lot more going on with Officer Peters and my sister Alexia at the time of our terrible descent than I could've predicted. And more, too, than they had bargained for, I'm sure.

The last we heard from the young officer was his chilling whisper, "The ghost!" and so I had assumed that the ghost was once again rising up to scare him away. Or it was going to come scare us away. It had, it seems, other plans.

The air had become frosty cold, Officer Peters told me later, a still calm running through the trees. But he said it felt less scary than the first time, and more like he was about to witness something amazing, the birth of a star or the rising of the moon in all its wonder.

The Indian ghost, bathed in a blue light, rose instead. It didn't have an angry or frightening look on its face, but a noble one, and Officer Peters felt drawn to it. This was beyond his imagining. He never thought he would feel this way or want to come closer to the apparition instead of running away.

With a gesture of his hand, the ghost beckoned him, and Officer Peters, almost as if he were gliding over the wet grass himself, started out of the trees and across the plain towards him.

It was spellbinding, other-worldly, he said, but not in a dreadful way. It was thrilling, fantastic, and he felt almost happy as he got closer and closer. But then, when he was almost to the first trench in the ground, the first digging, the expression on the Indian ghost's face changed.

It went from solemn and proud to sad, almost mournful. He gestured to his right and started gliding in that direction. Officer Peters followed.

Around the edge of the grounds which looked like nothing more than a half-started garden, with small and large trenches dug here and there, they moved. Officer Peters thought they were going to head out onto the vast plain that led to the ravine and the river, but instead, the ghost hooked back to where the ground started to slope up gently at first, up toward the library and where we were.

There was an area of dense undergrowth, a dark blotch of green and black in the night that the Indian now pointed to, when, all of a sudden, his eyes met squarely with the rookie cop's and they filled with a sudden and fierce rage. His mouth opened, and the Indian spirit let out such a shriek that it nearly stopped Officer Peter's heart. Then, it stood there, face returning to normal, as if it was listening, waiting. Suddenly, it bolted forward, drawing forth its tomahawk. But, it passed right through Officer Peters and surged up the hill.

The young man, despite all his fears, ran after it. If the ghost was headed for Shilah and me, he had to warn us, do something! But, as he scrambled through the trees, he saw an incredible sight.

A red glow appeared over the top of the hill and shot towards the Indian ghost that was streaming at it. In a brilliant flash that lasted only a split second, the two collided, red and blue beams silently exploding together and then they vanished and were gone. The dark of night poured in quickly to fill the void.

Out of breath, Officer Peters felt a dawning start to come upon his mind, like he was realizing a great secret which had been eluding him all along. But something interrupted this revelation. It rose up from behind a boulder at the base of a tree in front of him, unmistakable in its shape and its menacing blackness, his shadow!

How else can you describe it except that it was like having your best friend turn against you, not once, but over and over again? Every day, since he had made that fateful pact with the gypsy woman at the fortune-telling booth at the fair, this constant companion was out to get him.

Whether it twitched a little, grew larger unexplainably or made sudden movements to remind him that it had a power all its own, or whether it did more obvious, ominous gestures, it never left him alone. It never let him forget that his shadow had become the shadow of Death, and at some time, any moment, it would claim his life.

This night, at the other side of the Indian burial ground, Officer Peters fully believed it was that time, the end. The shadow rose up, arms raised above it, fingers stretching into black, talon-like claws, its ebony, smoke-like form spreading and widening, making it look wraith-like, like a massive black ship-sail ballooning over him, about to engulf him.

But the worst was the face. Its eyes and mouth, never visible until this night, were now blazing white hot, gaping at him with a raging, all-consuming fire.

And, despite his best efforts, despite all his intentions to make this the bravest night of his life, Officer Peters did what he almost always did. He collapsed.

"Help me!"

He caved in, cowered and curled into a ball on the mud-mingled pine needle patch of earth before the shadow.

"Oh God, help me!"

*   *   *

Alexia, on the complete opposite end of the emotional spectrum, was having the best of times. The call from the library manager, Gary Greystone, asking her to meet earlier than planned at the ice cream parlor off Main Street had been a happy change, a giggler, as she described it. Something that made her giggle.

Yes, it's nauseating, I know. And, here, I promise you that what you read is pretty much what she told me, and not anything I made up. She was always quite honest about her feelings, one of the things I admired most about my sister. Little did I know, I would add a few more attributes to that list before the night was over.

"Oh, this ice cream is delicious, better than I've ever tasted!" she told the handsome man across from her at the table near the big window with colorful letters displaying "Sam's Sundries & Ice Cream" above them, backwards. Of course, on the outside, the letters could be read normally, left to right, but they were sitting on the inside, where more than the letters could be considered backwards.

"The sweeter the person, the sweeter the taste, I always say," Greystone replied, all teeth and charm.

And here, Alexia remembered feeling nothing but happiness. She talked and talked, telling this unbelievable man a complete summary of her life up until the moment they first met when she responded to the online ad he'd placed for employment at the library. The most unbelievable part to her was that he was not only heart-stoppingly hunky (her words, not mine, thank you), he was a good guy, too. He actually listened, nodded, asked questions—he actually seemed to care.

And so, the hours passed without her even realizing it. She didn't even feel the vibration of her phone or notice the various text messages from family and friends:

How did the interview go? Home soon? – from our mom, six o'clock.

Is he as hunky handsome as he looks on TV? – from her best friend Lily, six fifteen.

Well, is he? – sent repetitively for the next twenty minutes, four times a minute. Yes, you guessed it, from best friend Lily.

Hello? Dinner's ready! – sent at seven o'clock from Mom.

Fine, just ignore me! – from faltering friend, Lily, at seven-thirty.

Nothing seemed to exist outside of the two-inch perimeter surrounding Gary Greystone. She followed him outside for a night stroll through the center of town, eyes always on him. It was a miracle she didn't fall into an open manhole or get hit by a car, she recalled, because she never looked where she was going, just always kept her eyes adoringly on her escort.

"And that's how I came to speak Italian, thanks to the olive oil smugglers I lived with for those two years and finally handed over to the authorities." He was finishing up a story as they came to the town square, passing directly beneath the statue of the Civil War soldier.

Alexia could remember hearing it make a grating sound at this point, though she never turned to look at it. But, thinking back, she felt almost certain that it had shaken itself a little, as if, beyond all belief, the statue was trying to move. Was it a knowing, annoyed glance that the library manager threw at the bronze soldier, or was it simply a troubled thought that crossed his mind, a glimpse into something darker that was going on at that moment that he suddenly seemed to be aware of?

She would find out soon enough.

*   *   *

As for Shilah and I, the whispers in the dark were our immediate concerns. They were female, the voices, and, from the differing tones and accents we could tell there was more than one source. But, it was so dark in the room, this odd-smelling confinement that Finnius Ardmyre had confined us to.

So, there was only one thing to do: Turn on our flashlights.

Have you ever felt like you'd rather not know if something horrible is waiting for you in the dark than turn on the light and face it? It was this heart-clutching feeling that made my hand tremble as I switched on my light.

What Shilah and I saw next was beyond our expectation, baffling at first to the senses. There weren't just two librarians in this big room that was the size of the whole downstairs of my house. There must have been fifteen women, at least. Some were as old as sixty, most of them younger, and all of them clinging to the outer walls; some sitting, some standing, hunched over, looking at their hands or fiddling with the edge of their dress or a random object like a gold locket or hair brush – all of them muttering and whispering, not to each other, but themselves.

And here's even the most shocking thing: They were all perfectly happy. These were cheerful little bemusements that they were uttering, like they were addressing someone before them or in their minds.

With a mouth-dropping look to one another, Shilah and I turned in a circle, illuminating every inch of the chamber, every woman until we found her. Thank God she was there! Miss Lucy.

Shilah hurried to her. "Miss Lucy! Miss Lucy!" She touched her shoulder and the woman looked up at her, hair straggly, face dirty and gaunt, as if she had lost thirty pounds since we last saw her. But still, she had that dreamy, elated expression in her eyes. Her lips turned into a sincere, joyful grin.

Here we go. We're finally going to get some answers, now. How she got here. What she's been doing all this time; who, if anyone else, is working with Ardmyre.

"So nice to see you!" she chimed, bird-like, though barely above a whisper, she was so weak.

"Oh, it's great to see you, too, Miss Lucy! We were so worried!"

"I'll get right to that, sir. Of course!" she said, with a nod and a dreamy smile.

And, here's where I realized it. She wasn't seeing Shilah, or me. She was seeing someone else, talking to someone else! But, who?

She immediately turned away and started flipping through an imaginary book in her hands, reading intently. Bewildered, we shined the light on the next one, someone much older than her, and she seemed to be deep in discussion—with the wall!

"Oh, no, my Jonathan would never pick up his dirty

clothes, not in a million years. He was a complete slob, took me totally for granted, even when he hurt his back in the mines and I took care of him for fifteen years. Yes, yes—they are so selfish, aren't they? You wouldn't believe what happened when we went to Philadelphia!"

I grabbed Shilah's arm and quickly pulled her away from the woman, worried that, whatever these women had, it was contagious.

"Shilah, get back! Over here!"

"Teddy, my arm!" she was alarmed, and I was, too; that's why I was pulling her so hard.

"Sorry! Sorry!" I let her go, once we were back at the door. "But, we can't—we can't let ourselves get sucked in!"

"What's wrong with them?"

"I don't—they're all like in their own trances, all in their own worlds. But, we have to—"

"Keep our heads, I know," she said, calming her breathing, holding my hands.

"Yes, and find a way out of here, like right now before Finnius Ardmyre brings this whole place down on us." I said, grabbing the handle to the door. It was locked.

Together, we slammed against it, tried to knock it loose, but it was too strong, and we weren't strong enough. We shone our flashlights high and low, looking for another way out. No good. There was no opening in the ceiling, no rock chute or air duct in the wall.

"Tools, tools!" I said, and we made our next search one of every corner and inch of the walls, in and around the babbling women. My heart ached for them, as I tried to get around them, "Excuse me, Ma'am." They were so ragged and weak looking, and so completely unaware of the danger they were in. I knew it was the work of powerful evil, here, and it made me sick, scared and angry all at once. "Could you just step to your left?" I asked, trying to move a woman in a worn and dirty evening dress.

"Yes, I'd love to dance!" she said, not even looking at my face, but still grabbing my hands and pulling me into a waltz through the center of the room!

"Shilah!" I shouted, and she must've heard the surge of panic in my voice, because she ran over and separated us quickly.

Out of breath, we ran back to the door. I leaned against it. "It's hopeless," I said. "I'm sorry, Shilah."

"We haven't tried calling for help," Shilah said. I could see the fear creeping into the corners of her steady eyes. She was trying hard to fight it back, I could tell.

I had to be strong for her, I knew it. I couldn't let her down again. "Okay," I said, "But that never works, you know that."

We turned and pounded on the door together, and shouted things like, "Hey, help! We're stuck in here!" or "Help us! We're in here! Somebody!" And, of course, my personal favorite, the long drawn out, "Heeeeelp!"

Exhausted, we leaned back against the door together. Shilah was biting her lip.

I noticed the hinges on the door, and made them my next focus. "We have to pop those hinges, somehow," I told her. "Don't worry, I'll figure out—"

"Heeeelp! Please help us!" Shilah cried, the fear completely overtaking her now, and I knew it was the voices of the women, the constant chattering, clucking and chuckling, along with the feeling that any moment, we'd hear the loud boom of an explosion and the ceiling would cave in on us.

Shilah fell into my arms, and she was trembling. "It's okay," I tried to assure her. "Don't waste your breath anymore. We're going to get out of here, you and I, don't worry. I got this, okay, Shilah. I got this."

Then, the most unlikely thing happened. Someone pounded on the door, on the other side of the door! A voice called to us, "Hey, are you there!? Are you in there, Teddy, Shilah!?"

We nearly exploded with excitement. It was Officer Peters!

"Yes!" we shouted, banging on the door again, jumping up and down. "In here! In here!"

"Stand back!" we heard his slightly muffled voice call. "Back away from the door!"

Shilah and I immediately took two steps back, shining our flashlights in unison on the wooden door and handle. Everything grew silent for a moment, and I couldn't even hear the voices in the dark anymore, I was so focused on that door. Shilah clutched my hand in anticipation.

The handle jiggled! And then, Crack! The whole door shook. Again, Crack!

"He's breaking through," I gasped. "Yes! Officer Peters!"

Over and over, the door jolted, until the wood between the handle and the door split and we could see the pointy end of a pick-axe burst through. It disappeared and suddenly, with a BOOM!, the door slammed in and there he was, our rescuer, with dust trailing all around him, miner's pick-axe in hand, glowing in the light, Officer Peters. "I'm here!" he shouted, totally out of breath. "I'm here."

We ran and hugged onto him, laughing so hard, we were so surprised, ecstatic and relieved all at once.

"Oh, Officer Peters!" Shilah said.

"You did it!" I beamed. "You came for us!"

We backed away as he gasped for air, grinning from ear to ear. "You don't even know!" he said, leaning on the busted doorframe. "Hold on, before I die, here!"

He took a moment to catch his breath, and he went on. "You wouldn't believe it, Teddy. I thought I was a goner for sure. This was it, the night I was meant to go. But no, I was meant to find you, both of you, to help you."

"What happened?" I asked, knowing we should be running for our lives, but also knowing he needed to compose himself before we could go anywhere.

"I'll tell you more, later," he said, "but all I can say now is that my shadow is back, the good one, and the bad one's gone, thanks to my sister. And thanks to the advice you gave me, Teddy."

"What advice?" I said, "I never—"

"Well, you're here, aren't you?" he said, clasping my shoulder.

Shilah's grin was contagious between us, and I couldn't help but smile. Something told me we were going to be all right.

"All right," I said, "let's get out of here. All of us."

"All of you?" he asked.

We promptly shined the light on the rest of our odd group.

"Ooh—oh. Wow." He said.

"It's all right, right?" Shilah asked. "You can get us all out the way you came?"

"Uh, yeah. Yeah, sure," he said, still struck but what he was seeing.

"Hey," I said. "How did you find us in the first place?"

"What?"

"I mean, how did you even know we were down here?"

"Oh, the Indian. The Indian ghost. He showed me."

Shilah and I looked at each other. It was our turn to be stunned. "What—how?" I stammered. "I thought he was—"

"Oh no, no," Peters told us. "He's good. Turns out, he's really good. He showed me an entrance to this mine shaft that was overgrown completely with bushes and nearly covered by rocks. Took me a while to cut and push my way through, but I did. I just knew I was meant to, you know? And then, after going along for a while, I heard your voices. I couldn't believe it, but I heard you guys."

I barely heard this last part, I was still stuck on the gaping hole in all of my theories that this revelation made, nearly drowning in the deafening roar of the icy, waterfall-like question that poured into it, raging in my mind. "If—if the ghost isn't the vampire, then--" I could barely get the words out, turning to my friend who seemed to share the same, horrifying thought.

Shilah finished my question, breathlessly. "Who is?"

17
WILL THE REAL VAMPIRE PLEASE STEP FORWARD? UM, ON SECOND THOUGHT...

Alexia later told me that it was his smile, really, that was his undoing. She began to notice not just how white it was, but how perfect and easy it shone. Too easy. Gary Greystone, she realized, was not smiling at her at all. Somewhere, buried in the back of her mind, the truth emerged.

He was smiling at himself. It wasn't a true, sincere grin, not at all. He didn't see deep into her eyes, appreciate her uniqueness, her inner beauty like she had first thought he did. No, it was the reflection of himself in her eyes, she realized—this was what he was gazing lovingly at.

And once this miniscule mention of the truth crept into the corner of her consciousness, the words I had told her back home on the staircase, sounded, almost like a trumpet in her mind: "You deserve a whole lot better than him. A million times better!"

Alexia blinked. She realized, dizzy all of a sudden, that she had no clue where she was. The face that she had been so caught up in, with that handsome, charmingly chiseled brow and chin, and dark, mysterious eyes, was gone. She was in a forest of trees. It was later, definitely night now.

She breathed in the cool air, looking around, trying to clear her mind, to figure out how she had gotten from her stroll through the town square to here, this—

"Oh!" she gasped, catching herself before falling backward. She realized, much to her shock that she was standing on the edge of a square, black hole in the ground, just dug right there into the forest floor. A hatch was open on the other side of it.

Then she saw beyond it to the shed. And there he was, but not alone. A tall, brooding man faced him, both inside the open doorway, engaged in a heated discussion. She recognized this other man immediately as the much-loathed mortician, Finnius Ardmyre.

"No, it's not that—" the tall embalmer was saying. "I swear to you!"

"Because if I questioned your obedience, Ardmyre, the others will certainly do so as well," Greystone told him, but not in his normal, airy, almost sing-songy voice. It was harsh and coarse and sinister-sounding. "And you know they will be less patient than I have been with you thusfar. Much less patient."

"I have no problem killing the boy, and the others," the mortician said, almost desperately. "I simply have to press this button," and he held up a small gadget, a detonator with a glowing yellow button. "But I'm saying, the girl will be too much—from the same family. It's too suspicious. The boy and his friend can be explained-- but if she's down there, too, I don't know if I can explain it. She's under your control. Let her go in the woods, and she'll eventually find her way home, won't remember anything."

Alexia covered her mouth. She knew exactly who they were talking about, and it froze her very heart with fear.

"But, I want her, don't you see?!" the library manager, who clearly wasn't just a library manager, hissed at Ardmyre. "I need her life force, just like the others. You'll find a way to avoid suspicion, fade into the shadows, like you've always done. It's what you do, and this is what I do. I will not be denied this, you understand me?"

Everything became clear to my sister at that moment. The hole in the ground. The detonator. The boy and his friend, and the others. It all fit together, but it was the sight of two objects on the ground that solidified the chilling truth for her: our walkie-talkies, crushed and broken, barely visible in the moon-spattered dark.

She, who was normally afraid of plastic spiders, my sixteen year old sister, made a decision at that moment, she later told me. She had to do something, or all of us would die. And she knew exactly what she must do.

But, as if sensing something was wrong, Greystone turned his head toward her suddenly, and instead of being thirty yards away at the shed, he was immediately at her side, taking her hand in his with that smile, that creepy, awful smile plastered across his face. "My dear," he said, his voice still low and horrid-sounding. And his hand wasn't warm and tender like it had felt as they had left the ice cream parlor. It was icy cold, almost scaly to the touch.

Alexia remembered how pale his face seemed now, and how blood-red his lips were, curled into a self-satisfied snarl.

"Let me help you into your carriage, my darling," he said, guiding her to where a ladder was visible inside the hole, going down. "Up you go," he told her, so confident in his mind-control that he was utterly convinced she believed she was going up into some sort of fancy coach, instead of downwards to her doom.

Now you have to understand a little background here. My sister, at the age of ten, had been convinced she was going to be the world's next big movie star, the next Meryl Streep or Audrey Hepburn, or whoever. Day after day, night after night, for a year straight, she had practiced in front of her mirror, organized family performances-- in which she held the lead role, of course-- in our basement. Her aspirations were fatally cut short, however, when she failed to get a small part in a low-fat yogurt commercial, and she had given up, quit, just like that. Apparently, she wasn't convincing enough when, after her actor-mother handed her a fruity yogurt, she had proclaimed, "This is the happiest day of my life!"

But now, years later, standing on the brink of death itself, it became clear that all the time spent honing her craft had not been in vain. No, tonight, she would shine.

"Oh, my sweet Mr. Greystone!" she said, dreamily, touching his face and moving lightly toward the ladder. She was like a radiant, Southern belle. "What a wonderful man you are! So thoughtful, so loving and exciting and thrilling! This really is the happiest night of my life!"

The line would've sold a million yogurts that night, and it certainly sold the evil Greystone as he was drawn up in her, almost soaking in her radiating presence like it was the very fuel to the engine that drove him, fed his existence. He was enraptured, empowered, seething with almost carnivorous pleasure.

And then she pushed him into the hole. "Ahh!" he fell into the darkness with a startled cry.

Alexia quickly slammed the hatch shut on him with all her strength and then dove into the cover of the trees. She turned frantically to look at the shed.

Finnius Ardmyre came running out, detonator in hand. "Master!" he called, his deep voice pathetically tinged with fear. "Master?!"

At this point, Alexia grabbed a large stone and made her even bolder move. I wish I could've been there to see it, because I'm sure it was an amazing sight, one that would've had every schoolchild, every old woman or puppy or snail that was ever afraid of Finnius Ardmyre roaring with cheers of praise and adoration.

She, my sixteen year old sister, lunged at the poisonous tree of a man, driving the river stone right at his drooping head!

But she missed. He straightened up, he did, pulling away in time, and he whirled around, staring at her in baffled amazement. There was only one thing left to do. She threw the stone at his mile-long shin with a dead-on throw that would've made any softball gal jealous, and, as he howled in pain, she lunged for the detonator.

The two grappled for it, gigantic man and petite, sixteen year-old girl-- they both grabbed onto it and would not let go, like it was the key to life itself.

That's because it was. It was the key to our life, and death, down in the maze-like tunnels below.

*   *   *

We knew we had very little time to escape with our lives, but we didn't realize we would face an even bigger problem: the women. How could we get them out, get them to follow Officer Peters, Shilah and me to safety-- and fast?

They were still lost in their babblings, the noise of their voices grating on my nerves more than ever. Even the crashing of the door and the entrance of the now-courageous cop did nothing to shake them from the spell they were under.

"Hey!" I shouted at the top of my lungs. "We have to go!" Nothing. Not even a glance from the nearest prisoner. "We're going to die if we don't go!" Still no reaction. "Die! Do you hear me!? Die?!" I nearly fell over, totally out of breath and exasperated.

Shilah bent low, whispered intently in my ear. "Teddy, I got it," she said, that wonderful gleam in her eyes, the one that always said there was a ray of hope still left in any bad situation. "Hold their hands," she said.

"What?!"

"Teddy, listen! Finnius Ardmyre said that the power was in you, that you had it within you, and there's no doubt it is. You have the gift. You can see things, see a reality that no one else can! We need them to open their eyes and see the truth. Who else can make that happen but you?"

Before I knew it, Officer Peters and Shilah were running around the room waving their arms and shouting. They were like sheepdogs, herding the poor women from the corners and edges, to the center where I stood.

"Here! Here!"

"Move! Go!"

The female prisoners pressed in on me from all sides, like a gaggle of geese, a massive, maternal movement, and I didn't know what to do, it was so overwhelming, their voices clashing and strangling out each other's like a whirlwind of words, of passions and laughter and convictions of the heart that fought to be heard and understood. But, they were all for nothing, going to no one, nowhere and it nearly crushed my heart; they were so lost, so completely lost.

I did the only thing I could do. I grabbed the closest hand to me—it was Miss Lucy's—and, with my other hand, I clutched onto my medal amid the madness. Please, God, let them see!

And suddenly, Miss Lucy stopped talking. Her chestnut hair flew back as she breathed in so sharply, it stunned me to see the shock she underwent, and her eyes went wide with something I've never been so happy to see in all my life: revelation!

The librarian grabbed the hand of the woman next to her. Swoosh! Same reaction! It was incredible. She, in turn clutched the fingers of the lady beside her, and like a spiraling wildfire of truth, the revelation spread through all the women who, before I knew it, were all connected to me, with a hand on me or on the person who, through a series of others, held onto Miss Lucy whose hand was in mine, encircled in an icy-burning, fiery grip.

Then, silence. Beautiful silence fell on the room. And I knew in my heart they were free.

Through the crowd, I could see the tearful reaction of my best friend, the girl who seemed to see more truth in these situations than I could ever see. She grinned in relief and I shared that grin, shaking my head in amazement.

Then, a sob from a woman. Miss Lucy let go of my hand as she held hers up to her mouth. "Oh my," she said. "What did I do? What did I do?"

I knew immediately that I couldn't lose them to the next major enemy that came rushing to envelope them—despair. No, I knew this enemy from first-hand experience.

"Listen to me!" I called out. "Please. You must be so incredibly confused, so full of heartache right now. I know!

But, please, whatever brought you to this moment, whatever you think you did, it's not important! You have to forget it. Look ahead! Look at me! Who you are is not what you've done! It's not! It's so much more, so much! All the gold in all the mines of a million worlds couldn't come close to its value."

Shilah cleared her throat at this, and her look seemed to say, "That's great and all, but, the cave-in, remember?!"

"That being said," I told the women, steadying my voice. "We need to run, and we need to run now. Not in a panic!" I added as an audible fear rose up. "But, fast and orderly, follow Officer Peters—he'll get us out of here! Right?"

"Right!" cried the young cop. "Everyone, follow me!" And he ran out through the open doorway.

No one followed. Moments later, he came back, bewildered, desperate. "Please?"

"Go! Go!" Shilah cried. "We have to run!" And, all at once, the women charged poor Officer Peters, who seemed more afraid of this stampede than anything. He took off down the hall, the women pouring after him, a sea of worried, weak and tired faces.

Shilah and I followed out into the mine shaft, the girl taking my hand proudly. "You did it, Teddy."

"We did," I said, limping alongside her.

And we hurried out of the room that could very well have been our tomb.

Officer Peters led the exodus, calling out here and there, his voice rising strong and solid through the echoing tunnels. "Watch your step here!" "This way! Left tunnel! Left!" "Keep your head low!"

And we were making it, we were going to make it, I knew. I could feel the mounting joy welling in my heart. Everything was coming together.

And then, we heard it, the distant, heart-gripping Boom! that, together with a slight shaking of the tunnel walls, could only mean one thing: Everything was about to come down—on us!

18
THINGS THAT MAKE YOU GO BOOM!

Now Alexia hadn't lost. Don't misread me, here. She had been amazing, a valiant she-warrior princess and an honor to the name of Gyros.

The problem was, those detonators were just so darn touchy.

Here's what happened. The foul, murderous man who fought with my sister for the gizmo that was set to trigger a death-blow explosion below, this dealer in the deceased made a critical miscalculation. He let go with one hand and pressed his leathery black glove into my sister's face, thinking he could peel her away easily, with brute force. He pushed and pushed.

What he didn't realize was that this girl had teeth. She sunk them clean into three of his fingers with a sickening crunch, and he roared in a high-pitch like a man suddenly on fire. Alexia slammed into him with all of her weight, throwing him off balance and causing him to fall onto his back like a felled, deadwood tree.

Thanks to time and the ages, destiny or divine preparation--whatever you'd like to call it, there was a good-sized rock that had decided to live in the exact spot of the forest floor that Finnius Ardmyre's head fell toward. Slam! He was out cold, unconscious.

Amazing, but true! My sister defeated the foul, fabled Finnius Ardmyre.

But the detonator, still caught in the motion of the man's descent, went flying into the air. Alexia dove for it. Time went on hold.

She slid through the pine needles, arms and fingers outstretched. Again, I wished I could've been there to see it. And I'm sure I would've cheered right along with all the rest of the forest creatures, the stars and the moon, as she caught it! She actually caught it.

Unfortunately, in doing so, she pressed the yellow button.

KA—and I'm sure you can guess the next part—BOOM.

Have you ever been in an earthquake before? It's not a fun feeling. Normally, you kind of rely on the ground to not let you down. It's supposed to stay where it is, do its job, right?

Well, with the ground trembling beneath her, my sister stood in utmost horror, holding the triggered detonator, and gasping at what had been done.

And here's what the explosion had done. It set off a rolling cave-in starting deep within the mines where the explosives had been placed, and working its way outwards. We were, of course, doing the same.

So, it was up to us to outrun the roaring rock, collapsing wood and crumbling earth that filled in the passages behind us.

It was a heart-pounding race, with the oppressive, suffocating dust clouding our vision, eclipsed only by the dreadful feeling that any moment, the lights would go out, for good.

Then, the women stopped. They crowded up in front of Shilah and I, and we shouted, "Go! Go!"

"Hurry!" I looked back, flashing the light behind me to see the cloud of dust and earth filling in the long passage moving like a tidal wave.

They started to move again, but slower, and we quickly came to realize why. The ground had fallen out in front of us, a gap of nearly ten feet that led to a treacherous fall below, and Officer Peters had managed to shove a fallen beam across the divide. He was reaching out from the other side, helping the ladies, one at a time as they came across the beam to him.

"Keep moving!" he shouted over and over after them. "The end is just up ahead. Don't stop! Don't stop!"

Shilah looked at me as the last lady made it across the beam and we came to it ourselves. She knew this would be near impossible for me to cross alone with my hurt leg. "Together!" she cried at me as the earth gaped behind us, its massive mouth yawning to engulf us.

"No! It's not safe! Can't risk two people!" I shouted back, fearing our combined weight would be the end of us both.

Officer Peters waved frantically from the other side. "Come on! Come on!"

"Go, Shilah!" I told her, shoving her to the beam.

"Not without you!" And she grabbed my hand and pulled me with her.

It was unbelievable, the agony of the terror. We wanted to run, but we had to keep our balance, and yet the whole place was caving in! And, with my injured, throbbing leg, it was so hard to keep myself steady. Without, Shilah, I wouldn't have been able to make it. That was for certain.

"That's it!" she kept saying. "Almost there!"

But we weren't even halfway across. The tunnel filled in behind us, dust and rock crumbling on our heads, choking our lungs, stinging our eyes.

"That's it!"

"Hurry!" Peters cried, stretching for Shilah.

Then, the beam dislodged. And we fell.

"No!"

But the cop caught Shilah's arm and I caught her leg, and we hung like a human chain over what I was sure would have been an even worse fall than the notorious open pit mine plummet. This theory was about to be tested.

Officer Peters could barely get the words "Hold on!" out when the roof came down on us.

"Ahh!" Shilah's scream was blotted out by the chorus of the cave-in, as she shared my third and final fall of this ill-fated adventure.

Down, down we plummeted, rock and earth our fellow journeyers through the darkness, down into a depth I felt strangely peaceful about. I found myself, not blacking out or overcome with shock but oddly passive as my body dropped, and I felt like I had entered the image of a Gustave Dore' etching from a coffee table book of *Dante's Inferno* that my mom had put out one year—only no wing-tipped angel would come to brace my fall. They chose not to stop Shilah's descent either.

Instead, a natural phenomenon did the job. Splash! The frigid water was both a terrible shock and a joyous kiss of life as we both plunged into what was clearly an underground river. It was a miracle that no large rock had crushed either of us or knocked us unconscious, but as we shot down this watery, subterranean channel, I knew it would take a few more miracles to get us out alive.

"Teddy!" Shilah cried, not too far from me.

"I'm here!" I said, but a wave choked me for my efforts. "Stay under as much as you can!" I sputtered. "Roof may be low! Duck, Shilah!"

Even though it was pitch black, I felt certain my prophesy was upon us, so I dove under the surface, my hands, chest and legs scraping against some rocks, and it was only just in time I discovered as I reached up and felt the solid stone roof now only inches above my head.

I swam through the insane numbness and watery blindness, lungs straining, heart racing with a thousand desperate fears. Would I ever be able to surface? Was Shilah okay? What about Officer Peters? Was he buried alive?

It seemed an eternity, my passage through the low, churning channel, and I almost lost all hope, all sanity—*it's over—she's gone! We're lost!*—before the end, unable to swim, unable to keep conscious, when my shoulder slammed into a boulder and I ricocheted upwards. I broke the surface, the wide open surface!

Breathing hugely in relief, I heard the coughing of Shilah, could see her form only a few feet from me, as something as wonderful as the air that rushed into my lungs filled the cavern: moonlight!

It came from up ahead where it looked like an offshoot broke from the main channel. Shilah was headed right for this. "Swim for it!" I shouted, pounding my near-dead limbs as hard as I could.

But Shilah wasn't swimming for it, I realized. She was swimming for the side wall of the river. I swept by her. "Shilah!"

She clung to the rock, panting, crying.

Panicking, I feared she was too weak to hold on and she'd just sink to the bottom.

"Come on!" I cried, and then quickly adjusted as the current swept me away from the side channel back into the deep, dark main river that led to only God knew where—and Jules Verne, of course.

Luckily, or maybe it was the last in a series of miracles that I was being given, but an outcropping of rock was there for me to hold onto, and what was even better was the beam that had fallen in before us, was caught against it. I gripped the wood, and scrambled to clutch onto the rock.

Then, I saw her. Shilah had let go, but she hadn't gone down, she went out, too far out from the wall, caught in the current that wanted to feed her, like a maiden sacrifice into the watery mouth of the earth.

"No!" And, I pushed with all my might on the beam, shoving it toward her. "Grab it, Shilah! Grab it!"

The end of the beam was lost in darkness. There wasn't a word or a cry or a shout from my very best friend in the world. Only the hungry, deadening roar of the black current.

I was pushing with all my might wedging myself with all the strength that I had left to press the beam against the rock, to keep it from being swept away. And, I was trying with all my heart not to cry, not to give up hope, dying with every ounce of my being to see that spark of hope that she always had to offer, alive and well in her emerald green eyes.

Instead, I saw a hand.

"Oh, thank God!"

And another small hand, and the straggly hair and forlorn face of my dear friend as she climbed, slowly, agonizingly, hand over hand up the beam and toward me.

"That's it!" it was my turn to shout. "That's it, Shilah!" And the tears did come, only they were tears of joy as she got close enough for me to grab her wrist and pull her in to me, to safety as I let the beam go on its own journey into an abyss we were never meant to see.

We held onto each other, shivering, coughing and crying in relief, and then, instinctively, knowing we didn't come this far to freeze to death, we pushed on through the side channel.

It led, after a swim that was like a cruelly unnecessary page added onto forever, to a place I had almost given up hope of seeing ever again. I can describe it in a word: Out.

But, can you believe, and is it even possible that once we were out, soon enough, I found myself wishing we were back in!

19
WHEN SPIRITS COLLIDE – YOU BETTER HAVE INSURANCE

There's no greater feeling than coming out of the depths of a subterranean river and into the free, fresh air of night alive with the hooting of owls and rustling of leaves and the crackling of stars above like embers in an eternal campfire. I hope everyone gets to experience this at least once in their lives. Although, not under these circumstances!

At the side of the river that cut through the Walters ranch, Shilah and I came out of a small cave, swimming into a pool of shallow water. It was tucked into the wall of the ravine, overhung with rock, a narrow, dark mouth that was most likely never noticed before—at least not in our time.

We were glad we had found it, though. Super amazingly

glad, if that string of words could even come close to capturing how happy we felt.

The water was warmer in the river pool, but still cold, and we hurried onto the shore. And we collapsed. Happily, marveling at what we had been through, we lay there. Though it was cold out and we were shivering, the deep numbness of our limbs soon began to wear off and it was nice to regain feeling, remember what fingertips actually felt like.

After a few minutes of recovering our breath and senses, the rest of the world and its heavy, immediate problems came back to us at the same time. I sat up, "We have to get—"

"—to the burial ground," she finished, sitting up at that moment, too.

We climbed to our feet and I started forward, looking upstream to get my bearings, but Shilah put a hand on my shoulder, held me back. "Thank you, Teddy," she said.

This surprised me. "For what?"

"You saved me," she said, and I could tell she was fighting back her emotions.

I wanted to say, *hey, you've saved me in so many more ways, I can't even begin to count them right now. Let's save this for a time when we can list them all out and you'll see what an amazing gift you've been in my life.* But, all I could say was, "Yeah, you're a really bad swimmer. Don't let yourself get sucked into endless underwater river channels next time, okay?"

She laughed, hitting me on the arm, and I laughed too, starting upstream.

Our laughter would fade all too quickly, though.

We knew we had to get back to where the mine shaft came out near the Indian burial ground, had to help however many women had made it out in time and aid in the rescue of those who hadn't. We expected they would be near hysterical, some badly injured. We hoped that we would find Officer Peters right there in the midst of them, helping or getting help himself; but deep down we expected to hear that he was unaccounted for, that he was still trapped in the mine.

What we didn't expect was a two-fold calamity. We were a lot farther from the burial ground than we had imagined. We climbed up the ravine and made it onto the plain, but we must have been at least two miles downstream from where we needed to be. And, the second, even more sickening revelation: we were not alone.

It came as a cold chill spreading across the tall grass that we plodded through, our soaked clothes clinging to us and suddenly becoming even more frigid.

I stopped, and Shilah stuck close to my side.

It was an unnatural, evil wind that swept over us, tilting every blade of grass down toward us, and not just from ahead of us, but from every direction, from all sides.

"Teddy?"

"Stay close to me."

She gripped my hand with trembling fingers. "What-- what do you see?" she stammered.

"You don't wanna know."

For, the red glow of the all-too familiar beast that had haunted me, hunted me for months was now emanating from the grass ahead of us. Slowly, it crept closer, and I spun in a circle, holding my friend close, looking for the way out, but there were more crimson, glowing entities on the plain, all closing in on us.

"Demon dogs. A whole pack of them," I told her, my voice surprisingly steady.

"What do we do?" she asked.

But there was nothing to do. My backpack was long gone.

We had no weapon at hand or in sight to fight these foul creatures off with. Yet, oddly enough, I felt a strange sort of peace envelope me, even as the menacing forms drew nearer and nearer.

"The only thing we can do," I answered my friend, breathless. "Hope."

At that moment, a bloodcurdling, hissing sound rose up around us, and we looked to see the grass at our feet wither and shrivel into brown, lifeless strands. The sickness spread, leveling a wide circle, at least fifty feet around us, and in doing so, it revealed at least nine of the deadly hounds of hell, claws dug into the earth, savage teeth and fiery eyes bared at us.

But there was something more, someone more, a figure coming out of the shadow as if stepping out of a wall of darkness ahead that he himself created. It was the very step of his foot that had caused the earth to cringe and the soil to choke and kill its own fruit.

The moon made it evident who this figure was, though I half-expected it in my mind before his face became visible: Gary Greystone.

"It's over, boy!" he called out, striding confidently toward us, almost to the ring of red that ensnared us. He stopped and held out his hand. "Your fate is sealed," he said, his voice no longer the charming, empathetic voice that had held all the newscasters smitten over the last months. It was the voice of pure evil. "Let the girl come to me, and I will spare her life."

I felt Shilah's grip become like steel, and it all made sense to me at that moment now. Of course, the vampire was Greystone. I should've seen it from the start, the way his eyes, his very presence seemed to soak in the attention of everyone around him and feed off of it, especially that of women.

"Teddy—no," Shilah could barely find her voice to say.

"She stays with me," I told him, remarking even to myself at how unafraid my voice sounded, how bold and strong. "You can't have her!"

"Oh, can't I?" the vampire snarled back.

"You have no power over her, no power here!" I answered.

And he laughed immediately, a mocking, caustic, bone-chilling laugh that turned into a commanding shout in a cryptic tongue as he thrust his hand out, pointing at us. The closest beast to him sprang forward, closing the distance between us with mind-blowing speed.

"Behind me!" I shouted, pulling Shilah behind me and raising my hand out in front of us, all I could do, though it seemed so futile, like nothing.

And yet, all seemed to slow, as what sounded at first like a chorus of angelic voices filled my ears.

The savage, jagged jaws and razor sharp claws came down on us.

And I knew, as fast as my eyes could register it, that it was not the sound of the angels, but a different otherworldly war-cry that I heard. An Indian war-cry!

And the ghost of the Indian we'd seen weeks ago on this very same plain soared from my right and crashed into the demon dog just as it was about to hit us. And he drove it into the decaying earth, sliding with it for ten feet.

All at once I realized that this is exactly what had happened on Halloween night. The Indian ghost hadn't been charging at us. He'd been racing for the beast that came at us from the other side. When I had ducked down and closed my eyes, I had most likely missed their collision.

But, I didn't miss this one. It was like two planets had slammed into each other, and Shilah and I were thrown back in the resulting blast of energy and radiating sound. We rolled up to our feet to see the Indian rolling with the great beast, grappling it, shoving its jaws away while trying to crush it with his muscular arms.

An infuriated cry came from the throat of the vampire, and the worst happened. The rest of the hounds of hell charged us.

"Heyaaaah!" cried the Indian ghost, and he paused in his battle to throw something back to me. It gleamed in the moonlight as it soared my way, hilt first, a hunting knife made of finely chiseled and sharpened stone.

I thought, like the ghost, it was nothing more than ephemeral spirit, that it would just pass through my hand, but I reached for it nonetheless, and I caught it!

Just in time, I turned to slash out at the first monster to reach us, and it howled in agony, driving into the earth and skidding away from us. The Indian was beside us now, slashing his tomahawk this way and that, fighting alongside me, and it was a glorious feeling, to be able to strike out at the very creatures that had held me captive, bound by fear for so long.

But, we were not enough, not fast enough, and it looked like we were going to be overrun by the vicious hounds, when a cry, similar to the one the Indian ghost had let out earlier, although louder and from multiple throats, rose up and came at us suddenly.

This glorious sound filled my ears as an amazing sight filled my eyes. A dozen Indian ghost-riders, on the bare backs of glowing wild horses thundered across the plain!

They crashed through our mêlée, striking down the ferocious hounds, and I shouted in joy as I slashed away with them. "Yes! Ha!"

Help had arrived. It was from the most unlikely of sources, but it was here!

Then, even as I started to feel the burning, joyful sensation of victory grow over me, I heard a sound that smothered it, the sound of my best friend crying out in pure terror.

I looked up and instantly plunged through the mix of horses, flashing weapons and reeling hounds to see, nearly a hundred feet away, the vampire rushing away across the plain, pulling Shilah with him. They were moving so swiftly it seemed the girl was flying behind him, like a kite, with both feet off the ground.

"Teddy!"

"Shilah!" I started after them, but even if both my legs had been perfectly normal, there would have been no catching up to them, they were so far away. "No!"

And then he was beside me, the Indian ghost whom we had first seen and who had first saved us at the Indian burial ground. He took a look at the situation and then, hefting a long spear with a jagged jade head on the end, he tilted his head back and seemed to call out to heaven itself.

Then, with Shilah and the vampire nearly half a football field away, the Indian ghost handed the spear to me!

I wanted to shout, "What're you thinking! I can't do this!"

But, for some reason, his confident gaze, and this peace inside me told me that I could. I took a step forward, hefting the heavy spear. The vampire pulled Shilah toward the trees, almost reaching them, almost reaching their cover.

It was now or never. I took two quick steps forward and launched the weapon. It seemed to soar with a life of its own, splitting the plain, the night sky itself, racing over the distance between fate and destiny itself, and struck right through the center of the fleeing vampire who, in turn, exploded in a blast of scarlet light and disintegrated into nothingness.

Shilah turned to me in shock and relief as the last of the demon dogs fell at the hands of the Indian spirits around us, their canine forms dissolving into the plain.

I breathed in amazement and joy. It was over. We had won.

Then, I collapsed to the ground.

The Indian ghost, still emanating the soft blue glow, as if a child of the moon itself, knelt beside me. I sat up. There was so much I wanted to say, wanted to know as I searched his eyes. They were so noble and strong, and yet there was still a deep sadness there.

What do you say to a ghost, though?

Turns out, I didn't have to say anything. He held out his hand to me. I placed mine in his, and instantly, more than words could ever convey, with a surge of energy, I saw, I felt what he wanted me to know.

We went together, to an age past, to a forest that seemed identical to the one near us, only younger, wilder—and I saw him there, moving through the trees, a bow in one hand, his spear in the other. He looked much younger, like a teenager not much older than me, very proud, and I could feel also that he was very angry, too. Deep down inside, there was so much rage, it frightened me.

The Indian knelt now, and I saw that he was right beside a fallen deer with an arrow through its heart. He looked proudly at his kill, but then his head jerked straight up and whipped to the side.

I followed his gaze. A large, black creature on all fours moved through the shrubs at the ankles of the pines to our right. It was a massive wolf.

My heart raced.

The Indian, unafraid, was like a statue. Not seeming to even breathe, he watched the wolf.

Yet the wolf was moving away from us, going in the other direction.

The Indian raised into a crouch, hefting his spear. This would be an even greater kill than the first. His eyes gleamed.

But then, something changed. It came over his face with the nearby sound of laughter. The laughter of women. Again, I followed his gaze. Further on, past the wolf, barely perceptible through the trees we could see women splashing in the waters of the river, washing clothes at the shore. They were white women.

And this was where my fear turned to panic. The wolf was headed right toward them.

Do something! I wanted to cry out, but I had no voice and no presence in the scene, either. Helpless, I was just a bystander, watching as the Indian straightened up, his face set like the coldest steel, and he turned and walked the other way!

It was only moments later when the sounds of the women's screams of terror, mingled with the bloodthirsty roars of the wolf, filled both our ears, a sound I would never forget.

And, suddenly, I was back on the plain, looking into the eyes of the Indian ghost. There were tears now in the older, sadder eyes, and now I knew why. He had not forgotten either.

He squeezed my hand tighter and I tried to convey with my own eyes, my thanks, my appreciation for his help, his bravery. If he had been waiting all these years for a chance to make up for what he had done; if he had been imprisoned by the agony of the fateful decision he had made all those decades ago, there in the forest when he let the wolf go, then I hoped with all my heart that he had found it this night. I hoped that he could finally be free.

He seemed to know what I was thinking. A peace came over his face, and the light of a deep joy looked to begin its triumph over the sorrow there. He nodded and released my hand to stand.

I stood too. And Shilah was at my side now. She held onto me as I held onto her. And we watched as the Indian ghost put his hand over his heart.

We could see the other ghostly riders on their horses in a V-formation behind him. One horse was empty. It was waiting for him.

Shilah and I put our own hands over our hearts, returning the gesture.

Then, in a flash, he turned with two great, exuberant strides and leapt onto the back of the waiting steed. Together, they all reared and turned to gallop off down the plain, a thundering sound that shook our hearts more than the earth, and a beautiful light that filled our glistening eyes as they lifted into the sky and faded one by one, our friend the very last, into the stars themselves.

20
DIGGING OUT AND DIGGING IN

It took until midday the next day for the rescue workers to dig Officer Peters out of the mine shaft. It turned out, he had not made it out in time. But, all of the women had. They were alive. They had injuries, yes, but nothing major, and would recover soon enough. The big question was the rookie cop.

The world watched and waited. Either way, if he was dead or alive, the young officer, our friend, would be remembered forever in the town, and beyond, as a hero.

This was quite a shift from being the most cowardly cop in the state of Minnesota, and even as we waited to see, with bated breath if he was all right, I could not help but marvel at how things had turned out.

"There's always a way," I said out loud, more to myself than to Shilah who sat beside me at the rescue camp just outside of the Indian Burial Ground perimeter. Mr. Walters was nearby shouting orders to some people who were bringing water to the workers.

"What?" she asked. "Were you talking to me?"

"I was just thinking," I said. "Sometimes you think things are impossible, that they won't get better."

"And then you're standing on the other side," she finished the thought, "and you look back and realize, yeah, the way was there all along."

At this moment, a round of cheers went out from the entrance to the mine. We both shot out of our chairs to see a great commotion among the rescuers. There were newscasters and reporters pressing in to get the answer to the question everyone wanted to know, yet maybe, outside of his parents, no one wanted to know more than Shilah and I.

We started running toward them, fighting our way through. Then, a hush fell over the crowd, and in my heart, I feared the worst: Were they were silent because he was? Deathly silent?

But, thankfully, it was just because they all wanted to hear the young man's first words as he came into the light of day, carried on a stretcher by two men. "What's for lunch?"

*   *   *

His mouth full of stuffing and turkey, Officer Peters said, "And Captain Rogers even gave me a promotion! The youngest detective on the force, if you can believe it!" He knocked over a wine glass with his left arm that was in a cast. "Oh, sorry!"

It was a week and a half later, Thanksgiving Dinner at my house, and everyone was there, around the table. My family, Shilah, her mom, and the young cop. It was the second day after his release from the hospital with two broken legs and one broken arm. But certainly, his spirit was nowhere near broken. He was the happiest I'd ever seen him.

"To Officer Peters!" my dad said, raising his own wine glass. "We all owe a great deal to you, young man."

Everyone else saluted and raised their glasses filled with wine, water and apple juice accordingly.

"He didn't wash his hands before leaving the bathroom," Leah, our little informer told us after downing her juice.

Peters' face turned red. "I—I—"

"Leah!" Mom chided her. "That's not at all polite, young lady."

Shilah and I exchanged a laugh, and Doug and Alexia couldn't help but smile, too.

"What about Alexia?" I said, looking at my sister who had risen to the top of my list of people I most admired, "for single-handedly defeating the evil, Finnius Ardmyre with her awesome street-fighting skills?"

She shook her head, wanting to be remembered least of all in this affair, I knew, as a kung-fu action star. She had actually been quite traumatized after the event, and was only now starting to be able to joke about it. "It's you Teddy," she smiled. "If you didn't believe in me…"

"You're right," our town hero said, still holding his glass up. "It's true. I couldn't have done it—I wouldn't have done it without these two, here," and he gestured to Shilah and I. "They gave me hope, helped me believe I could."

"Here, here!" came the loud, Irish brogue of Father McReedy who came in through the back door with Sister Margaret close behind him. He lifted a bottle of wine. "Happy Thanksgiving, everyone!"

Dinner was outstanding with so much good food, so much talk and laughter, and I ate enough to feel like one of the floats in the Macy's Thanksgiving Day parade.

Afterwards, Shilah and her mom were out front on the phone, talking to some family on the West Coast, so I was about to crash on the couch next to my dad and brother who were debating with the old parish priest about which football team was best this year, when I decided, for some reason, to go out back for some fresh air.

Maybe I wanted a moment alone to reflect on things, to sort out just how much I was thankful for this year: my family, Shilah, and Officer Peters for sure, and Father McReedy who helped me get back up when I'd fallen.

I stepped out onto the back porch. One of my mom's canvases was drying off to the left against the rail, and I smiled when I saw what it depicted. It was a painting of two crutches, formed into the shape of a cross on a hilltop with the sun rising behind it, radiating through it.

"All our weakness made strong," she'd told me, when I first saw it the other day, and she gave me a kiss. She was a remarkable woman and I was so thankful for her steadfast love, along with that of my father.

I thought of how much family love really mattered in this world, thought of how Officer Peters' sister, her presence, her belief in him had saved him, helped him overcome the shadow of death that plagued him for so long. He had later told Shilah and I, during one of our many visits to his hospital bedside, the rest of the story of what happened that night at the mine entrance. The shadow had risen to swallow him whole, it seemed, but something else was with him there in the dark terror. The thought of it actually brought tears to my eyes, once more, just like when he told us about it the first time.

It was so simple, so pure and beautiful. A single, shimmering butterfly danced above him as he cowered on the ground, the very creature that had been his sister's favorite in all the world. Now, he knew that it was how she chose to come to his aid, weaving through the dark and piercing right through the center of the shadow.

Watching through tears, Officer Peters recalls that all he could think of was not losing his sister again, and so he leapt to his feet and charged, crying out with fear-crushing fury, brimming with courage, and diving right into the shadow that shattered it into a million splinters of blackness that showered down and then retreated like worms into the damp forest soil. And this was how he had gained his freedom, so he could come and save our lives.

Next, I thought of the Indian ghost who came to our rescue at the very end, and hoped he was with his family now. The entire, final incident on the grassy plain was something Shilah and I had decided not to share with anyone else at the time. Why, you ask?

Well, with Finnius Ardmyre in a federal penitentiary awaiting trial, we didn't want to cloud the waters with anything extra right now. So when the hardly appreciative FBI Agent, Lorna Wood, had questioned us, seemingly more upset that we had succeeded without her help, we kept to the physical facts only.

The captive women, aside from their presence there in the mines, provided little extra for these facts. None could remember much at all, and so it was being speculated that Ardmyre had used mind-control tactics to put them into their mentally-deprived state. We didn't want to give credit to the now-missing library manager, Gary Greystone, who, thanks to Alexia's testimony, was under full suspicion of being Ardmyre's accomplice, if not the mastermind of the crime.

Since we knew Greystone was not punishable under any

worldly court of law, we wanted to make sure Ardmyre got the full rap he deserved. The fact that Shilah had managed to take my digital recorder from my backpack and capture most of the mortician's rantings from our fated walk through the tunnels that night would turn out to be a nice nail in the coffin of this case. Ardmyre was crazy, the jury would decide. He wanted to add us to his collection of captives, and we would have been buried with them all had Officer Peters not come to our aid.

Of course, it went so much deeper than that. Not a night went by since, that I didn't go over his words to us below the earth before sealing our doom.

Were the forces of evil, the vampires, going to be out to get me from now on, because they thought I had a power, or some sort of key to a power, that could defeat them all? If I let it, the notion that I was a target for millions of vampires would make me sick and paralyzed with fear. So, I decided not to let it.

I decided to trust that I would be able to face whatever came my way; and no longer alone, not on my own, but with the amazing help I knew was available to me. I was grateful that heavenly help had come through for me again. It seemed I was needed to live and to fight another day.

What would that next fight be? I didn't know, but as I stepped out of the enclosed porch and onto the wooden steps leading down into our yard, I had a feeling that I had come face to face with my answer.

There, standing in the glow of the twilight light, was the towering, larger-than-life statue of the Civil War soldier from the town square.

Whoah! How did it--? I blinked in stunned silence, thinking that maybe I'd eaten a bad cranberry or someone was playing an elaborate prank on me, when the statue supplied the answer.

Not with a word, though. It took a step toward me. It actually moved!

And its eyes, though made of bronze, were filled with brimming emotion, a mournful depth of ages filled with secrets that I knew, if I asked, would be revealed to me. It looked, with such severity at that moment, like it wanted nothing more in this world than to tell me those secrets. The question that pounded my heart in the bated silence between us was borne of exhaustion, I knew, but also, I admit, a lingering, persistent fear, as night itself waited to dawn once more.

Did I want to know?

MICHAEL SORTINO

ABOUT THE AUTHOR

Michael Sortino lives in Scottsdale, AZ with his wife, four kids, and two dogs. He writes for film projects, education, corporate and television. His greatest love is writing and telling stories that his kids and other kids of all ages can enjoy.

COVER ART & DESIGN by **Fr. Anthony Sortino, LC.**

Printed in Great Britain
by Amazon.co.uk, Ltd.,
Marston Gate.